P9-DJL-843

*Unable to help herself, Betsy reached out and stroked his cheek, fingering his solid, square-cut jaw, the faint bristle of his beard.*

His gaze locked on hers, stirring up something deep within her, and any reservations about getting involved with him flew out the window.

As he lowered his mouth to hers, his musky, masculine scent assaulted her better judgment and set her mind swirling in a maelstrom of desire.

This was so not what she'd planned, but it no longer seemed to matter.

He brushed his lips against hers—once, twice, a third time. Then he took her mouth and claimed it.

Dear Reader,

I don't think there could be a better setting for a Christmas romance than Brighton Valley, Texas.

Within the pages of the book you're holding, you'll meet Dr. Betsy Nielson, a dedicated physician at the Brighton Valley Medical Center. Betsy, who was betrayed by her ex-husband, is facing the holiday season head-on, determined to focus on her work and her patients. But when a tall, dark and handsome mugging victim is brought into the E.R., battered and suffering from amnesia, Betsy is tempted to do something she's never done before—get involved with a patient. Still, can she trust a man who doesn't even know his own name?

I don't know about your life, but mine gets busy and hectic during November and December. So I try to take time for myself and relax whenever I can. One good way I relax is by curling up with a book whenever I get a chance. I hope you'll do the same.

Merry Christmas and happy reading,

Judy

# UNDER THE MISTLETOE WITH JOHN DOE

## JUDY DUARTE

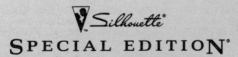

**SPECIAL EDITION®**

Published by Silhouette Books

America's Publisher of Contemporary Romance

If you purchased this book without a cover you should be aware
that this book is stolen property. It was reported as "unsold and
destroyed" to the publisher, and neither the author nor the
publisher has received any payment for this "stripped book."

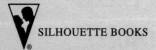 SILHOUETTE BOOKS

Recycling programs
for this product may
not exist in your area.

ISBN-13: 978-0-373-65562-5

UNDER THE MISTLETOE WITH JOHN DOE

Copyright © 2010 by Judy Duarte

All rights reserved. Except for use in any review, the reproduction
or utilization of this work in whole or in part in any form by any
electronic, mechanical or other means, now known or hereafter
invented, including xerography, photocopying and recording, or in
any information storage or retrieval system, is forbidden without
the written permission of the editorial office, Silhouette Books,
233 Broadway, New York, NY 10279 U.S.A.

This is a work of fiction. Names, characters, places and incidents are
either the product of the author's imagination or are used fictitiously, and
any resemblance to actual persons, living or dead, business establishments,
events or locales is entirely coincidental.

This edition published by arrangement with Harlequin Books S.A.

For questions and comments about the quality of this book please contact us
at *Customer_eCare@Harlequin.ca.*

® and TM are trademarks of Harlequin Books S.A., used under license.
Trademarks indicated with ® are registered in the United States Patent
and Trademark Office, the Canadian Trade Marks Office and in other
countries.

Visit Silhouette Books at www.eHarlequin.com

**Printed in U.S.A.**

**Books by Judy Duarte**

## JUDY DUARTE

always knew there was a book inside her, but since English was her least favorite subject in school, she never considered herself a writer. An avid reader who enjoys a happy ending, Judy couldn't shake the dream of creating a book of her own.

Her dream became a reality in March of 2002, when Silhouette Special Edition released her first book, *Cowboy Courage*. Since then, she has published more than twenty novels.

Her stories have touched the hearts of readers around the world. And in July of 2005, Judy won the prestigious Readers' Choice Award for *The Rich Man's Son*.

Judy makes her home near the beach in Southern California. When she's not cooped up in her writing cave, she's spending time with her somewhat enormous but delightfully close family.

To Janet Elmore, who reads every book I write.
This one's for you, Janet! I hope you like it, too.

## Chapter One

A Texas honky-tonk was the last place Jason Alvarez could have imagined himself being on a Wednesday night. But here he was, turning into the graveled driveway of the Stagecoach Inn.

It had been a long day, starting with an early morning workout at the gym, followed by an executive board meeting at Alvarez Industries. After having a business lunch with his brothers at an upscale restaurant in downtown San Diego, he'd flown to Houston on the corporate jet, then rented a car and made a two-hour drive to Brighton Valley.

He'd stopped once he'd reached the sleepy little town and asked where he could find a local watering hole. Apparently this backwoods cowboy dive was the nearest and the most popular.

The parking lot was only half-full, though, so finding a spot was easy. He pulled in between a white Chrysler

LeBaron with a missing taillight and a beat-up Chevy pickup with gun racks and pasted decals in the rear window that said the driver's name was Eddie and his passenger was Arlene.

Without even stepping inside the place, Jason had a feeling he wasn't going to like the music or fit in with the crowd. But he was on a mission, and personal preferences didn't matter.

So he shut off the ignition of the rental car, a black Cadillac Seville, and unhooked his seat belt. But he didn't get out right away.

Instead, he reached for the bottle of aspirin he'd tucked into the pocket of his sports jacket and opened the child-resistant cap. Then he threw a couple of tablets into his mouth and chased them down with the remainder of the bottled water he kept in the built-in cup holder.

His head was aching again, a result of the concussion he'd suffered earlier this week in an automobile accident.

He'd been using the Bluetooth device on his cell phone when it happened, distracted by a business matter, his mind on everything but the road. His Mercedes had zipped right through the intersection, T-boning a minivan and injuring a pregnant blonde as well as her little girl.

Jason, who'd suffered only a concussion and some minor bruises and lacerations, had rushed to help the other victims, calling 9-1-1 as he did so.

Then he'd stood by helplessly as firemen used the Jaws of Life to remove the woman from the driver's seat and the paramedics treated the child. The police had questioned him, and he'd clearly been at fault—the officers had known it, and Jason had known it.

When they'd told him he should be checked out by EMTs and taken to the hospital just to make sure he was okay, he'd declined treatment, saying he'd see his personal physician later.

The memories were just as clear now as they'd been on Saturday afternoon—the shattered glass, the twisted metal, the moans of the pregnant driver, the cries of the frightened little girl.

The guilt had just about sucked the life out of him, and he'd finally confided in Mike, his older brother, telling him that he thought he should take a leave of absence. He'd just wanted some time to sort out a few things—and he wasn't just talking about the guilt he was dealing with because of the accident. He wondered if the concussion he'd suffered might have done something to his thought process because he was questioning a whole lot of things the past few days, things he'd never even blinked at before.

But Mike, who was facing a false accusation and a few legal problems of his own, had said, "Don't worry about it, little brother. Accidents happen, and what's done is done. I've got the company attorneys on it already."

Yeah, right. The same attorneys who were already at work on the allegation of sexual harassment against Mike—a charge he was probably guilty of. And one that would make the family look bad.

Jason raked a hand through his hair, glanced into the rearview mirror at his haggard reflection, then shook his head and blew out a sigh. No matter how badly he felt about the tragic accident he'd caused, his brother had been right about one thing—there wasn't much he could do about it after the fact.

But the guilt and the memory of the whole surreal scene was something he'd have to live with for a long, long time.

Now, as he got out of the car and hit the lock button on the key-ring remote, he glanced at the orange-neon open sign that hung off-kilter from a front window of the cowboy bar. He sure hoped his hunch had been right, that Pedro Salas had returned to his hometown. And that the former employee would agree to come back to California to testify on behalf of Mike and the entire Alvarez family—if he needed to.

To make the request even more appealing, he'd been told to offer Pedro his old job back—if he wanted it.

Of course, that smacked of a bribe, as far as Jason was concerned. And if it was, he'd have to deal with the reality of his oldest brother's fall from grace—at least, in Jason's eyes.

He supposed that a lot had to ride on just what Pedro had to say.

As Jason's leather soles crunched upon the graveled parking lot, he hoped that he'd find Pedro here, drowning his sorrows in a bottle. It certainly seemed likely, because drinking on the job had led to Pedro's discharge from Alvarez Industries. And that was why looking for him in one of the local bars seemed to be the logical first step.

Jason had always liked Pedro. He'd sympathized with him, too. The poor guy had lost his wife and son in a fire back in 2002 and had never gotten over the loss.

It was easy to see, especially now, how a man might want to escape painful memories and grief any way he could—at least for a while.

Jason was tempted to shake his own demons, too— the nightmares of sirens, the blood, the cries. The fact that his focus on business, rather than the road ahead, had caused the whole thing.

Hell, even his ex-wife had accused him of being so obsessed with work that he was incapable of loving anyone more than he loved Alvarez Industries.

At the time, he'd wanted to argue with her, but a piece of him had been afraid that she might be right.

As Jason stepped into the darkened bar, music blared from an old jukebox and hoots of laughter tore through the room, its air heavy with stale smoke and booze.

For a moment, it seemed as if he'd stepped onto a movie set, and he couldn't help pausing in the doorway for a beat, watching the people cut loose and have fun. But the sooner he found Pedro, the sooner he could go home.

When he spotted an empty table, he made his way across the scuffed and scarred hardwood floor. He'd hardly taken a seat when a cocktail waitress with bleached-blond hair approached. He guessed her to be in her late thirties, but it was hard to tell. Nicotine, booze or a hard life had a way of aging a person beyond his or her years.

She offered him a smile that failed to take the load off her shoulders. "What'll you have?"

He wasn't sure if a bar out in the sticks would carry imported beer. "Do you have Corona?"

She nodded. "You want lime with it?"

"Yes, thanks." He watched her walk away, but not because he fancied her. Instead, he noted the way she rolled her shoulders as if her back ached.

When she returned, she set his drink in front of him.

"I'm looking for a man named Pedro Salas," he said. "From what I understand, he was born and raised in Brighton Valley and had planned to retire here."

"Is he an old guy?" she asked.

"About forty-five or fifty."

"That's pretty young to retire." She glanced at Jason's sports jacket, probably noting the expensive fabric, the stylish cut. "Well, unless he's rich or something."

For the first time, he began to realize his hunch might have been wrong, that Pedro might have stayed in California and found another job. But the last time they'd talked, he'd had such a yearning, wistful look in his eyes when he'd talked about ranches and horses that Jason made the assumption that he'd run home.

"He mentioned that his father used to work on a small spread in this area," Jason added. "He grew up on the place and went to school here."

She seemed to give it some thought, then slowly shook her head. "I'm sorry. The name doesn't ring a bell. And there're quite a few ranches in these parts— both big and small."

She could have left it at that, but instead, she hung back, as though hoping for an invitation to sit with him, to chat awhile longer, to rest her tired feet.

But he wasn't up for company. And even though he wasn't a loner or a drifter by nature, he'd just as soon finish his beer and then find a room for the night.

"Can I get you anything else?" she asked.

"No, thanks. I'm good."

"Well, my name's Trina. Just give me a holler when you want another beer."

"I will."

As she went on her way, he took a healthy chug of the ice-cold Corona and scanned the bar crowd, most of whom didn't appear to have noticed him.

There was a part of Jason that just wanted to find Pedro and get a declaration that the attorneys could work with. But rather than flying home immediately after completing the task, it seemed a whole lot more appealing to hang out in a small town like this for a while, in a place where no one knew him or his family, where he'd have the peace and privacy to sort out a few things.

But he couldn't afford to take the time away from the office long enough to lick his wounds.

He supposed Renee, his ex, had been right about him. He *was* too focused on business. But his family had always been important to him, and his loyalty ran deep. Of course, he wasn't going to cry in his beer over the divorce—or the accident. Not here, not now.

Instead, he decided to make his way through the honky-tonk and ask people about Pedro.

Ten minutes later, he hadn't learned squat. So far, no one seemed to know the man he'd been looking for. He wasn't sure if his lead on Pedro had been false or if people had collectively clammed up in a small-town effort to protect their own.

Either way, neither the aspirin nor the beer had taken

the edge off his headache, and he decided to call it a night.

He reached into his pocket for his wallet and pulled out a ten-dollar bill. After leaving it on the table for Trina, he got to his feet.

He'd no more than started for the door when a tall, lanky cowboy entered the bar, along with a short, stocky companion. Jason wondered if it was worth talking to either of them, but before he could make a move one way or the other, Trina approached the men.

When she faced them head-on, she slapped her hands on her hips. "Unless you two are carrying more than counterfeit bills this time, your money's not welcome here."

"You can't blame that on *us*," the chubby guy said. "We got 'em right out of the ATM down at the filling station."

"Yeah, *right*," Trina said. "Are you going to leave? Or do I have to call security?"

"You mean that scrawny old geezer you called last time?" The slim one laughed. "He couldn't throw my ninety-eight-pound granny across the room."

Chubby headed for the bar, clearly not listening to the waitress and apparently not worried about whoever provided security at the honky-tonk.

"I told you to get out of here," Trina said, raising her voice above the din of music and all the barroom chatter.

Ignoring Trina's words and tone, Slim stood tall and threw his chest out. "What do you care, baby? You don't own the place. And that quarter tip we left after your lousy service was the real deal."

Jason scanned the cowboy joint, looking for security or for a sign that someone would back him up, but the jukebox blared with a lively beat and the hoots of laughter continued. So finding someone to step up to the plate and take his side wasn't likely.

When Slim grabbed Trina's arm and gave it a jerk and a twist, Jason's protective instinct kicked in and he made his way toward them.

"Why don't you guys just back off and leave the lady alone," he said.

"She ain't no lady." Slim released his grip on Trina and turned to Jason. "And who in the hell are you?"

"Just a man who doesn't like to see women mistreated." Jason preferred to use his head instead of his brawn, but that might not be an option tonight.

Fortunately, at that point, a big burly guy stepped in—a bouncer, it seemed.

And this one wasn't a scrawny old man.

At about six-foot-six and probably weighing close to three hundred pounds—nearly all muscle—he could have taken on a couple of linebackers for the Houston Texans without breaking a sweat.

"I don't want any trouble," the bouncer said, "so you guys will have to take your squabble outside. Or better yet, go on home and call it a night."

Slim mellowed right out and tossed the man a chipped-tooth grin. "We were just havin' a little fun."

The bouncer crossed his muscular arms, his biceps stretching the cotton fabric of his T-shirt to the limit. "Yeah, well, take your fun somewhere else."

"Come on," Slim called to his buddy. "Let's go

on down to Larry's Place. The help is a lot friendlier there."

Apparently, Chubby saw the wisdom in Slim's suggestion, and they both headed out the door like a couple of docile pups, their tails tucked between their legs.

When they were gone, the bouncer turned his gaze on Jason, as though he wasn't all that welcome here, either.

"It's okay," Trina said on Jason's behalf. "This guy hasn't been any trouble. He stepped in to defend me while you were in the stockroom."

Jason wasn't sure what he'd been expecting from the bouncer—a thank-you, maybe. But he didn't get anything.

He did, however, make a mental note to check out Larry's Place tomorrow. He certainly wasn't going to follow Slim and Chubby anywhere tonight.

"Do you know where I can find a motel?" he asked Trina.

"The Night Owl is a couple of blocks down the street."

"Thanks."

"It doesn't look like much on the outside," she added, "but it's clean and the beds are soft."

He didn't ask how she knew that. Instead, he thanked her, then strode toward the door. On his way out, he reached into his pocket for the keys to his rental car and headed for the parking lot.

A streetlight at the road was flickering, yet it gave off just enough light for him to see someone near the driver's door of his vehicle, as if trying to break in.

"Hey!" he called out, picking up his pace.

Chubby looked up, but he didn't appear to be too concerned about being caught in the act.

Where was Slim?

Footsteps sounded behind him, but before he could turn around, his head exploded with pain—then everything went black.


The E.R. at the Brighton Valley Medical Center had been unusually quiet, even for a weekday night, but Dr. Betsy Nielson wouldn't complain.

While doing her internship, she'd learned to use her downtime wisely, so she went into the break room and poured herself a cup of coffee.

But as usual, the peace and quiet didn't last long.

Dawn McGregor, one of the nurses on staff, poked her head in the doorway. "Dr. Nielson? We've got an ambulance on the way with an unconscious man in his late twenties–early thirties. He was robbed and beaten up outside the Stagecoach Inn."

Betsy took another sip of coffee before pouring it down the sink. "What's the ETA?"

"Three-and-a-half minutes." Dawn handed Betsy a list of the man's vitals that had been relayed to the hospital via the radio in the ambulance.

Betsy glanced at the readings, making note of them, then headed for the triage area.

Moments later, the automatic door swung open as paramedics rushed the victim into the E.R.

Showtime, Betsy thought, as she met them partway and began a visual assessment of the patient while they all moved into the exam area.

Blunt-force trauma. Lacerations and bruises…

As she moved in closer, she realized that the man had gotten some of his injuries before today. One wound near his hairline already had sutures.

She guessed them to be about a week old—maybe less.

A bar fight? she wondered, coming to that conclusion because of where he'd been when he'd gotten this beating. That and the fact that the Stagecoach Inn had had more than its share of scuffles lately, resulting in their hiring an ex-marine as a bouncer.

She smelled alcohol on the patient, but it wasn't as though he'd been stewing in it all day, like a lot of the other drunken Stagecoach regulars who ended up in one of the E.R. exam rooms during one of her nighttime shifts.

"What happened?" she asked Sheila Conway, the head paramedic, as she ordered lab work and an MRI.

"He was hit from behind and rolled. No wallet, no cash, no credit cards on him. And he's completely out of it."

His clothing, while bloody, was expensive and stylish. Definitely not the usual patron of the Stagecoach Inn.

"Anyone know his name?"

"Nope."

"What about his vehicle?" Betsy asked. "Did they check the registration?"

"If he had a car, it might have been stolen. From what we were told, all the cars in the parking lot have been accounted for."

"Didn't anyone know who he is?"

"Apparently, he walked in alone, asked about a guy no one recognized, had a beer and left. But he didn't get far. Someone hit him with a tire iron and left him in a pool of blood. The bouncer found him and called us."

The patient moaned, and Betsy decided to quiz him. They had no idea of his medical history or allergies. Nothing to go on but what they uncovered here and now.

The police, who'd most likely been called already, would be here shortly. And they'd want to question him, too.

"Hi, there," she said. "How are you doing?"

Another moan. A blink.

She flashed a light into his eyes, saw his pupils— dilated. She'd be ordering that MRI stat.

When he looked at her through bloodshot eyes, she said, "I'm Dr. Nielson. Can you tell me what happened?"

He jerked and stiffened. His eyes grew wide and panicked. "How's the kid? Is she okay?"

"What kid?" she asked, wondering if a child had been in the vehicle that was stolen. She couldn't imagine someone being so negligent that they'd leave a youngster in the parking lot of a bar. But it happened.

"The stop sign," he said. "I didn't see it… I'm sorry."

He was rambling and confused. Did he think he'd been involved in a car accident?

She studied his pained expression, the raw emotion on his face, the concern in his striking blue eyes.

"You were robbed outside the Stagecoach Inn," she said, trying to shake the sympathy that drew her to him and was making it difficult to keep a professional distance. "What's your name?"

He stared at her blankly. Then confusion spread across his face. "I don't know."

In spite of the blood and dirt on his brow and cheek, he was an attractive man, and her heart quivered with the realization.

*Get over it,* she scolded herself. He was a patient. A victim. And a complete stranger.

"Do you know what day it is?" she asked.

A furrowed brow suggested that he didn't, and his eyes sought hers. "No, but the…kid? Her mom? Are they okay?"

"There wasn't anyone with you." At least that was the word she'd gotten. She looked to Sheila for confirmation.

The head EMT nodded. "As far as we know, he went in and out of the Stagecoach Inn alone."

Betsy returned her attention to her patient. "You were the only one hurt. And it wasn't a car accident. Someone assaulted you when you left a local bar and stole everything but the clothes on your back."

The tension in his expression softened, but only slightly. Then he closed his eyes and drifted off again.

The head injury could account for the temporary amnesia, and while she didn't suspect a fracture, she knew his brain had experienced some serious trauma tonight.

Betsy glanced across the gurney to Dawn, who usually worked the evening shift with her in the E.R. "Let's get an MRI and see what's going on."

The nurse nodded. "Anything else?"

Betsy issued the rest of her orders, and as soon as

Dawn left to make sure they were fulfilled, Betsy took another look at her patient.

She reached for his nearest hand, which just happened to be his left. He wasn't wearing a ring, wedding or otherwise.

It might have been stolen along with his wallet and other valuables, she supposed, but she didn't see an indention or a tan line. His fingers were straight, sturdy and they appeared to have been manicured recently.

She turned his hand over. Too bad she couldn't read palms. It would be helpful to know more about him—medically speaking, of course, although her curiosity was mounting. Who was this guy? And what had he been doing in a rip-roaring honky-tonk on a Wednesday night?

A hardened ridge of calluses marred his lifeline, suggesting that he might lift weights or swing a golf club regularly. Or maybe it was from gripping the handlebars of a bike.

His build, while sturdy and strong, seemed more in line with sports than with weights and gym equipment, but it was hard to tell.

*Who are you?* she wondered.

He appeared to be a city boy, so it was easy to assume he was a stranger in town—a tall, dark and handsome one at that.

She had a feeling that he'd be drop-dead gorgeous when he was in full form and had all of his senses about him. The kind of man who could even turn the most dedicated doctor's head.

Cases like this didn't drop into town or the E.R. very often, and Betsy was glad that they didn't. After her unexpected and painful divorce, she'd sworn off romance, especially with someone who might not be the man he pretended to be.

She released John Doe's hand, trying to shake her interest in him. The sooner she admitted him to the hospital and sent him up to the third floor, the better off she'd be.

The last thing in the world she needed to do was to befriend a man who couldn't even remember his name.

## Chapter Two

Betsy's shift ended at seven o'clock the next morning. But instead of going home, fixing herself a bite to eat and unwinding with a cup of chamomile tea as usual, she rode the elevator up to the third floor to check on John Doe.

Betsy took a personal interest in each one of her patients. Typically, after they left the E.R. and were handed over to other doctors, she was able to set her concern aside. But this particular patient had really tugged at her heartstrings and she wasn't sure why.

She supposed it was only natural to sympathize with a man who'd been robbed of his valuables, as well as his memory, even if the amnesia proved to be temporary.

When the elevator doors opened, letting her off on the third floor, she headed to the nurses' desk, where Molly Mayfield sat, her head bowed as she studied a patient's chart.

It was both nice and reassuring to see her friend and coworker on duty today. Molly was one of the top nurses at Brighton Valley Medical Center, but she only worked part-time. After marrying race-car driver Chase Mayfield and giving birth to their baby girl, she'd cut back her hours at the hospital. But it was great having her stay on staff, even if it was only two or three days each week.

When Molly looked up from the chart and spotted Betsy, she brightened. "I thought you were working nights this week. Did you change your schedule?"

"No, I just stopped by to check on a patient." Betsy rested her arm on the counter, next to a lush poinsettia plant, its red-and-green leaves a reminder that Thanksgiving had just passed and that Christmas was right around the corner.

Her gift list wasn't very long—only three people this year—but she put a great deal of thought into each present she gave, which meant she'd have to start shopping soon.

Her interest in the poinsettia didn't go unnoticed, as Molly smiled and leaned forward. "Isn't it pretty? Chase brought it the other day when he and Megan came by to have lunch with me."

"That was sweet," Betsy said.

"I know. Chase is always doing little things like that to surprise me."

"It's nice to see you so happy."

Molly grinned, her eyes sparking with love and contentment. "I never realized how much I'd enjoy being a wife and a mom."

At one time, Betsy had entertained thoughts of

motherhood, too, but not anymore. Doug Bramblett had seen to that.

Three years into their marriage, when she'd been wrapping up her internship, she'd found out that her husband was having an affair. She'd no more than come to grips with his deceit when she learned that the extramarital relationship he'd had with a receptionist at his office hadn't been the first.

Betsy had filed for divorce, then spent the rest of her internship trying to pick up the pieces of her once-perfect life. Then, two years later, Doug was arrested and convicted for his involvement in an insider-trading scheme.

Clearly the guy she'd once loved and trusted hadn't turned out to be the honest, loyal and ethical man she'd thought he was. But she pressed on by moving away from the big city to Brighton Valley, where the neighbors knew—and could vouch—for each other.

And now that she was here, her focus was on work, on the medical center and seeing it succeed.

"How are Chase and little Megan doing?" she asked her friend.

Molly's grin nearly lit the entire west wing. "They're doing great. And Megan just cut her first tooth. She's pulling herself up and taking a few steps. You ought to see her, Betsy. She's the cutest little thing."

"I'd love to. We'll have to get together soon." Of course, Betsy didn't have many free nights. With the financial situation at the hospital being what it was, they'd had to cut back on staff, and she'd been taking up the slack.

"Maybe, when you switch to working days, you can

come to dinner some evening," Molly said. "I miss not seeing you."

In spite of being friends, they had never really socialized. Betsy didn't have the time. In addition to her work at the hospital, her parents had moved into a nearby assisted-living complex. And as an only child, Betsy made sure to visit them regularly.

She'd been adopted when her mom and dad had just about given up on having a baby, and she owed all she was to them, to their love and emotional support. So every moment she spent with them now was precious.

Instead of commenting about how busy she was, Betsy smiled at her friend. "As a wife and a new mommy, I imagine your time is stretched to the limit."

"It is, but I wouldn't have it any other way. I can't imagine life without Chase or Megan." Molly closed the file she'd been reading and moved it aside. "So what—or rather *who*—brings you up to the third floor?"

"John Doe—unless his memory returned and he's going by another name now."

"No, he's not. From what I was told, he was pretty agitated about it last night. So Dr. Kelso sedated him."

"Is he sleeping now?"

"No. I was just in there a few minutes ago, and he was awake. But he's still not sure who he is."

"Which room is he in?"

"Three-fourteen."

"Thanks."

As Betsy made her way to John Doe's room and peered inside, she spotted him lying in bed, his head turned toward the window, revealing the gauze that covered the wounds he'd received from the assault.

His hair, which was a bit long and curled at the neckline, looked especially dark on the white pillowcase.

When he sensed her presence—or maybe he'd heard her footsteps—he turned to the doorway, and their gazes met.

He'd been cleaned up, but no one had taken time to shave him. The dark stubble on his jaw and cheeks made him look rugged and manly, completely mocking the soft, baby-blue hospital gown he was wearing.

"Good morning," she said, entering the room. "I'm Dr. Nielson. You may not remember me, but I treated you in the E.R. last night."

"Actually," he said, "I remember *that*."

"Being in the E.R.?"

He nodded. "Well, at the time, while looking up into the bright lights, I saw you and assumed I was standing at the Pearly Gates with a redheaded angel. But I never figured heavenly beings would be so pretty."

She didn't know whether he was serious, joking or flirting. It was impossible to tell from his tone or his expression. Yet for some crazy reason, her hand lifted inadvertently to feel for loose strands of hair that might have fallen from her brass clip.

"And then," he added, "in the middle of the night, before they drugged me—or maybe afterward—I saw you again."

"I'm afraid that wasn't me. I spent the early morning hours in the E.R., patching up a drunk who walked through a plate-glass window and treating a toddler for croup."

"I figured as much. The last time you appeared

over my bed, you were hanging out with a gang of lep-rechauns. I figured you were their queen."

"I'm afraid my days of running with the wee ones are over." She smiled as she moved closer to his bed. "By the way, the police came by the E.R. to question you last night, and I suggested they come back in the morning. Have they been in yet?"

"No, but it'll be a waste of their time. The only thing I remember is the color of your hair, those emerald-green eyes and the way everyone around you jumped when you gave orders. So it's nice to know that some of the crazy visions I had last night were real."

"I can only attest to the bright lights in the E.R. and barking out orders. The rest of those sightings must have been a result of the mugging or the sedative Dr. Kelso gave you."

"Maybe so." He studied her now, and as his eyes sketched over her face, her heart rate spiked and sput-tered—clearly not a professional response.

Time to exit, stage right.

Yet her feet didn't move.

"So how are you feeling now?" she asked, trying to gain some control over her hormones.

"I'm doing all right, I guess. My head's pounding like hell, though. And I can't remember anything. How long is that going to last?"

"The amnesia? I'm not sure. A few hours? A couple of days?" She didn't dare tell him that it could go on for a long time.

"Damn. That sucks."

She had to agree. She had no idea what she'd do if

she found herself in a strange hospital with no idea of who she was or how she'd gotten there.

"So what *do* you know about me?" he asked.

"Just that you were at one of the local honky-tonks, asking about a man."

"What man?"

"Somebody named Pedro. And for what it's worth, no one in the bar knew him."

He thought about that for a moment, as if trying to place the man or the reason for his search. Then he seemed to shrug it off. "What happened after that?"

"You had a beer and left. In the parking lot, someone decided to lift your wallet, but didn't want to risk a tussle with you. So they hit you with a tire iron and made sure you couldn't put up a fight."

She let him ponder that for a while, then said, "When the medics brought you into the E.R., you asked about a child and her mom. No one was with you at the bar. Could they have been witnesses?"

"It's possible, I guess. But you'll have to forgive me. I'm still drawing a complete blank."

"That's understandable. But you might want to pass that information on to the sheriff, just in case."

"All right." For some reason, she got the idea that he was used to giving orders. If so, being laid up was going to be tough on him.

"Anything else?" he asked.

She crossed her arms and tossed him a wry grin. "I'd venture to say that you're in your late twenties or early thirties. You stand about six foot tall or more and you're in good shape."

He was also one of the most attractive men she'd seen

in a long time, with broad shoulders and tight abs—as bruised as they were when she'd examined him—she couldn't help noticing. He also had eyes the shade of Texas bluebonnets, which was unusual for a man who appeared to have more than a little Latin blood.

"That's it?" he asked.

"Pretty much. You were well dressed and wore expensive clothing, so I think you've got a decent job—or a trust fund." Of course, Doug had taught her to be skeptical of men like that, so she added, "Then again, you could be a con artist."

"Yeah, well, apparently whatever money I may or may not have isn't available to me anymore."

Rather than answer, she gave a little who-knows? shrug.

He paused a beat, then sobered. "So you think that I was just passing through town?"

She doubted that he was a drifter, if that's what he meant. And the mystery about him, both medical and otherwise, intrigued her.

So did the spark of life in his eyes.

And the square cut of his jaw.

But she wasn't comfortable talking to him about her observations, when he might think that she found him attractive.

Okay, so he definitely was hot, and any woman who still had breath in her body couldn't help but agree.

Betsy wouldn't act on it, though. And if John picked up on those vibes, no good would come of it.

"Well," she said, backing away from the hospital bed. "I'd better head home. I've got to get some sleep because my next shift starts in—" she glanced at the clock on the wall "—less than twelve hours."

"Will I see you again?"

His tone, as well as the question, took her aback. And she didn't know what to tell him. In truth, there wasn't any reason for her to come back to see him, but she couldn't seem to bow out completely. "I'll stop by around dinnertime."

He smiled. "I'll look forward to it."

There went her heart rate again, and she struggled with the wisdom of a return visit. Yet she nodded, then turned and walked out of his room.

She wasn't exactly sure what had just happened in there. But she blamed it on a lack of sleep.

And a lack of sex, a small voice whispered.

Oh, for Pete's sake. Her self-imposed celibacy had been working out just fine. So why him?

And why now?

She'd be darned if she knew—or dared to pursue— the answer.

John Doe slept off and on the next morning, hoping that eventually he'd wake up with his memory intact. But so far, nothing had come to mind.

Just before lunch, Dr. Kelso came in to perform some kind of mental evaluation, this one more complex than what he'd had so far. John had passed most of it with flying colors. He had some basic knowledge, although he certainly wouldn't try his luck on *Jeopardy* or *Who Wants to Be a Millionaire?*

But memories of anything prior to his arrival at the E.R., anything of actual value, had been lost to him.

"So what's the verdict?" he asked the neurologist.

"Well, the good news is that the MRI has ruled out a skull fracture, but you have a cerebral contusion."

"What's that?"

"It's a bruise on the brain tissue," Dr. Kelso had explained. "I don't think you need surgery at this point, but we'll keep an eye on it. If it worsens, we may have to go in and relieve the pressure. But for now, we'll be giving you steroids to lessen any swelling."

"What about my memory?" he asked.

"You have retrograde amnesia."

"How long is it going to last? When will I remember who I am?"

"It's hard to say. The causes and symptoms of amnesia vary from patient to patient. And so does the recovery process. I'm afraid we'll just have to wait and see what happens in your case."

Great. "How long will I have to stay in the hospital?"

"That depends, too. I'd say at least a couple of days, maybe a week. But that could change if there are complications."

He wondered how he was going to pay the bill. Did he have health insurance? A job?

Of course, that was the least of his problems now. As it was, he was stuck in limbo—and in Brighton Valley—until his brain healed and his memory returned.

"I'll be back to see you later this afternoon," Dr. Kelso said. "In the meantime, get some rest."

There weren't many other options, John decided, as he settled back into his pillow, hoping to find a comfortable spot. Besides the outside wounds from the tire iron, his brain was bruised. No wonder his head ached.

As he dozed off and on during the afternoon, he periodically glanced at the clock that hung on the wall across from his bed, wishing that the hours would pass quickly. Dr. Nielson had said that she'd be back around dinnertime, and he couldn't help looking forward to her return.

Sure, she was an attractive woman, in spite of the blue scrubs she wore. He wondered what she'd look like dressed in street clothes—maybe a pair of tight jeans and a slinky blouse. A splash of makeup to highlight the color of her eyes. Her auburn curls hanging soft and loose around her shoulders.

But it was more than the redhead's pretty face and intense green eyes that appealed to him.

As he'd watched her leave his bedside this morning, he'd felt as if he'd just lost his best friend.

But why the heck wouldn't he? Besides his neurologist and the floor nurse, John didn't know—or remember—another soul on this planet.

And each time that dark realization struck, a heavy cloak of uneasiness draped over him, weighing on him until he was ready to throw off his covers, jump out of bed and tear out of this place.

But where would he go? What would he do? How would he support himself?

Did he have any skills? A degree? A job that was pressing?

He'd be damned if he knew.

Dr. Nielson had said that he'd been asking about

someone named Pedro. But who was the guy? And why did he want to find him?

Maybe he was a private investigator working on a missing-person case, but that didn't seem likely. For some reason, the *real* missing person in the whole scenario seemed to be *him*. And no matter how hard he tried to think or to focus on his name or his past, he drew a complete blank.

He didn't even know what day it was, although he suspected it was late November or December because of the Frosty the Snowman trim on the bulletin board in his room.

The Christmas season, he thought. A time for home and hearth, for family and friends.

Did he have anyone special in his life? Was there someone who'd been counting on him to come home last night? A wife? Kids? Maybe even a dog or a cat?

The questions came at him like a volley of rubber bullets, but he had no answers.

A sense of frustration rooted deep in his gut, making it hard to relax, to sleep, to heal. And no matter what he did, he couldn't seem to wrap his battered brain around anything. All he had were the details Dr. Nielson had given him, and right now, she seemed to be his only connection to the outside world.

No wonder he looked forward to seeing her again, to talking to her.

Maybe, with some time, a little rest and another visit from the pretty E.R. doctor, everything would start falling into place.

At five-thirty that evening, just before her next shift began, Betsy rode the elevator up to the third floor to look in on John Doe, just as she'd told him she would.

Again she pondered the wisdom of following up on a patient who was no longer her responsibility. But what was the harm in making one last trip upstairs?

As she walked along the corridor to the west wing, her rubber soles squeaked upon the polished linoleum floors, announcing her arrival. There was still time to turn around and head back to the E.R., with no one the wiser, but she pressed on.

Upon reaching the nurses' desk, where Jolene Collins was talking to someone on the telephone and scratching down notes, Betsy caught a whiff of the dinner cart before she actually saw it. Her stomach growled, reminding her that she probably should take time to pick up a bite to eat in the cafeteria before starting her shift.

In fact, maybe that's where she ought to be now, but it was hard to backpedal when she'd already come this far.

She could reach for her pager, check it and pretend she'd been called to another floor, but the hospital didn't get amnesia victims every day.

Or handsome young patients who piqued a single doctor's interest.

It was at that realization that she almost did an about-face, no matter how abrupt it might seem to anyone observing her behavior.

She had no business even imagining anything remotely romantic with a patient, especially John Doe, whose background was a complete unknown. After her divorce, she'd made up her mind to focus on work and to look after her aging parents, the loved ones who had never let her down—and who never would.

So she shook off the misplaced attraction to John,

telling herself that the brief visit would never amount to more than that.

As she neared John's room, she scanned the corridors but didn't see Molly, who was undoubtedly with a patient, which was just as well. There wouldn't be any need to come up with a good reason for her return to the third floor.

As Betsy reached the open doorway of 314, she spotted John sitting up in bed, his meal spread out on the portable tray in front of him.

"Hey," he said, brightening as he spotted her. "Finally, there's a familiar face."

She supposed that meant he was still struggling to regain his memory.

"How are you feeling?" she asked, returning his smile.

"Better, I guess." He pointed to the IV that dripped into the vein in his arm. "The stuff they're putting in here must be working. My head isn't aching quite as bad as it was earlier."

"That's good."

"But I still don't remember anything of substance."

"Do you remember anything at all?"

He shrugged. "I turned on the television earlier, and as I flipped through the channels, I came to a college football game. The USC fight song was familiar, and I knew the words."

"So you think you might be an alumnus?"

"Or I could be a dropout. Who knows?"

She made her way to his bedside and peered at his plate. "Roast beef?"

He nodded. "It's not as bad as I thought it was going to be."

"Actually, Brighton Valley Medical Center has a great cafeteria. I usually prefer to eat here more times than not."

"And where do you eat when you're not working?"

"At home."

"Where's that?"

Normally, she didn't offer her patients any details about her personal life, but for some reason, she felt like opening up to John. Maybe because she felt sorry for him. "I live on a small ranch outside of town."

"Oh, yeah? That surprises me."

"Why?"

"I don't know. You're a doctor, and I figured you for a place in the city and close to good restaurants and all the cultural haunts."

She laughed. "In Brighton Valley? You're definitely new in town."

"Which means there probably isn't any reason to post a picture of me on the back page of the newspaper and ask residents to call in if they recognize me." The smile he'd been wearing faded, and she figured that he'd been trying to make the best of a bad situation but wasn't having much luck.

"Well, we have some clues that we didn't have before. You might be from California. And you might have once attended USC."

His shrug indicated that her guess wasn't much to go on.

"What about you?" he asked.

"Originally? I'm from Houston. After my…" She

caught herself, realizing she didn't want to mention her divorce—certainly not with a stranger whose gaze was enough to set off a flurry of hormones. So she altered her explanation by saying, "Well, after my internship I had an opportunity to take over a medical practice in a small town, so I moved to Brighton Valley and worked with Dr. Graham until he retired."

"And so you liked it here and purchased property."

It was a natural assumption, she supposed. And there was no reason to set him straight, but she did so anyway. "I'd planned to get a place of my own, but Doc invited me to stay in the guesthouse at his ranch until I got settled."

They'd both thought it would be a temporary arrangement, but Betsy had never moved. She'd blamed it on being too busy to look for a house, but it had been more than that. Living so close to Doc had provided her with an opportunity to learn from an old-school physician who was a natural diagnostician and who was still making house calls up until the day he took down his shingle.

Sometimes, in the evenings when she wasn't on call, she would brew them both a pot of tea, and they would sit before the fireplace and talk. On those cozy nights, she would laugh at his anecdotes and soak up his wisdom like a child sitting on his knee.

She might have learned the modern methods of treating illness and disease in med school, but Doc had taught her how to deal with people—and not just the patients.

"Are you still living on his ranch?" John asked, as he shifted one of the pillows behind his back.

She nodded, and a slow smile stretched across her face as she thought of the little decorative touches she'd added to make her bedroom warm and cozy, the green-and-lavender quilt she draped over the foot of the bed, the picture of a lilac bush that hung on the wall. "Yes, I'm still there. And even though his guesthouse is just a little bigger than a studio apartment, it's home to me."

Sure, every now and then she thought about buying a place of her own, one that was closer to the hospital and to Shady Glen, the retirement community in which her parents lived. But even if she wanted to move, she'd have to rent at this point in her life. She'd used almost every dime of her savings to buy stock in the medical center—something very few people knew.

"And you have no plans to move to a place of your own?"

"No, not now. Doc is getting older, and his health isn't as good as it once was. Since his wife died, he's all alone."

"And you feel an obligation to look after him?"

"It's more of an honor." And she felt the same about looking after her parents, too.

"You're not only a good doctor," John said, "you've also got a good heart."

She wasn't sure what made her more uneasy—his praise or her self-disclosure—and she wondered if she ought to back away. After all, she didn't know this man from Adam.

"So," John said, connecting the dots, "in a way, you've become Doc's personal physician."

"I guess you could say that." She glanced at the clock on the wall, then drew up as tall as her five-foot-two frame would allow. "My shift will be starting soon, so I'd better go. I just wanted to check in on you."

"I like having my own personal physician, too."

That wasn't the impression she'd wanted to give him, but what did she expect? She'd stopped by his bedside for the second time today.

And if truth be told, her interest in him had drifted beyond that of physician-patient and bordered on female-male.

But she'd be darned if she'd admit that to anyone, especially to him.

She glanced at her pager, even though she hadn't heard a sound or felt a single vibration. "Well, I'd better go. Enjoy your dinner."

"Will you be back in the morning?" he asked.

Would she?

She shouldn't—and she hadn't planned on it.

Yet she found herself agreeing anyway.

## Chapter Three

Two days later, after closing up the cozy little house she'd called home for the past two years, Betsy strode across the yard to where she'd left her car.

The brisk wintry air and an overcast sky suggested a storm was on its way, so she turned up the collar of her jacket. Most women who worked a day shift would be ready to put on a pot of soup and batten down the hatches for the night. But not Betsy. She was heading to the hospital to start another twelve-hour shift.

As she reached the driver's door of her white Honda Civic, she spotted Doc walking out of the barn and heading toward her. Nearly ninety, his gait was more of a shuffle these days.

"You're leaving earlier than usual," he said.

She smiled at the man who'd become a mentor, a second father and a friend. "I want to check in on a patient before I start work."

"A child?" he asked, knowing that she had a heart for kids, especially those who were seriously ill or injured.

"Actually, it's a man who was robbed and assaulted outside the Stagecoach Inn Wednesday night. He's got amnesia."

"Oh, yeah?" The old man leaned his hip against her vehicle, as though intrigued by the case, too.

"He's a stranger in town," Betsy added, "but the expensive clothing he wore tells me that he has ties to a community somewhere."

"That's too bad. I had a case of amnesia once, back in the late seventies. A father of three fell off a railroad trestle near Lake San Marcos and damn near broke his neck. When he came to, he didn't know who he was or where he came from."

"Did he ever get his memory back?"

"Eventually. Once his wife reported him missing, police were able to put two and two together."

Betsy sobered. Did John have a wife? The possibility sent an uneasy shudder through her veins.

"So how old is this fellow?" Doc asked.

"My age or a little younger."

"How's he look?"

"Medically speaking? He's got a gash on his head that's healing. And his rib cage is bruised."

"That's not what I meant. Do you think he's good-looking?"

Uh-oh. So Doc was more intrigued by Betsy's interest in an adult male patient. But she'd have to put his mind to rest, even if she couldn't completely deny her budding attraction.

"I suppose he's handsome," she said, downplaying the fact that the current John Doe was drop-dead gorgeous. "I talked to Jim Kelso, the resident neurosurgeon, and he's planning to discharge him soon. He'll need to stay in town, I suspect. But at this point, he has no place to go or any resources."

Doc fingered his chin and furrowed his craggy brow. "That's too bad. Not only is the poor guy struggling with the memory loss and a lack of cash or credit, but he's also backed into a corner."

Betsy nodded, glad Doc seemed to think her interest in John was strictly professional.

Okay, so maybe it was a little of both. No one needed to know that.

"I thought I would talk to Sadie down at the Night Owl Motel. She might be able to give him a discount on a room."

"You can't ask Sadie to run a tab like that for a stranger. What if he isn't financially set? What if he can't pay for his keep?"

"I plan to cover the cost," she admitted. But Doc was right. They didn't know anything about John. Nor did they know how long he'd have to stay in town.

"Under the circumstances, I can't let you do that. You could be left holding the bag for a very long time. And your savings can't take another hit like that."

Betsy had received a solid financial settlement after her divorce, thanks to her ex-husband's innate ability to invest their money wisely. And she'd made a risky investment herself, one that had nearly tripled her funds overnight. Then she'd used the proceeds to buy stock in the medical center.

Doc had made a sizable investment in the facility himself. And with the hospital struggling financially… Well, Betsy wouldn't think about that now.

"Tell the patient he can stay here," Doc said. "I've got room in the house. And you and I can keep an eye on him that way."

Have John stay at the ranch?

Her heart ricocheted in her chest. Just the idea was…

What? Brilliant? Perfect?

Reckless?

"Knowing that he has a place to stay and a way to support himself ought to help put his mind at ease," Doc said.

It might put John at ease, Betsy realized. But the thought of John Doe living so close to her was doing a real number on her.

As one day stretched into a second, and then into a third, John still couldn't remember who he was or what he was doing in Brighton Valley.

His injury had been serious, and doctors were monitoring the contusion to make sure it didn't worsen. If it did, he would need surgery.

There were a lot of things he didn't know these days, but he was certain that he didn't want anyone operating on his brain. And so far, so good. He hadn't needed surgery.

Dr. Kelso had mentioned something about releasing him in the next day or so, which was great. But he had no idea where he'd go.

He'd figure out something, he supposed. He certainly

couldn't lie around in a hospital bed for the rest of his life. But God only knew what he'd do to support himself.

Footsteps sounded, and he looked up to see a dark-haired teenage girl wearing a pink-striped apron. She poked her head into his doorway and smiled. "Would you like a magazine or a book to read?"

John hadn't felt up to doing much of anything for the past couple of days, but it was much easier to concentrate now. His headaches weren't as intense and he was feeling more like himself.

Well, whatever "himself" meant.

So he said, "Sure, I'll take one. What've you got?"

She wheeled a small cart into his room, and he scanned the offerings: *Ladies' Home Journal, Psychology Today, People, Field & Stream...*

*Golf Digest?* For some reason, that particular periodical, with a head shot of Phil Mickelson on the cover, seemed to be the most appealing in the stack, so he took it.

When the candy striper left the room, he began to thumb through the pages, wondering if he'd been a golfer before the mugging.

If so, did he play regularly? Or had he just taken up the sport?

That answer, like all the others he'd been asking himself over the past two days, evaded him.

He had, of course, picked up a few clues to his identity. He knew the USC fight song, had an appreciation for college football and didn't much care for poached eggs.

According to one of the nurses, he had an imperious

tone at times, as if he was used to giving orders, rather than taking them.

And he *might* play golf.

But that wasn't much to go on.

As he continued to gloss over the pages in the magazine, he paused to scan an ad for a new TaylorMade putter that was gaining popularity. It looked familiar. Did he have one in a golf bag somewhere?

His musing was interrupted by a silver-haired, pink-smocked hospital volunteer who entered the room and announced that it was dinnertime.

She carried in his tray, and when she set it on the portable table, he studied his meal: grilled chicken, a side of pasta, green beans, a roll and a little tub of chocolate ice cream.

"Thanks," he said.

"You're welcome." She offered him a sweet, grandmotherly smile. "Can I bring you anything else?"

"No, I'm set." He paid special attention to his attitude with her, offering a smile—no need for her to think he was bossy—and waiting to pick up the fork until after she'd left the room.

Hospital food was supposed to be lousy, which was one more piece of useless information he'd managed to recall hearing at another time and place, but the food here wasn't too bad.

As he speared a piece of lightly seasoned rigatoni, he glanced at the clock. Dr. Nielson would be stopping by soon—at least he hoped she would. He was getting tired of watching TV, and her visits were the only thing he had to look forward to.

Something told him that she didn't have a professional

reason to stop and see him. And if that were the case, he wondered whether it was a personal one.

He sure hoped so. Her visits had become the highlight of his day. Of course, he figured that even if he was back in his real world, her smile would be a welcome sight.

His first postmugging memory was of her pretty face, those vibrant green eyes and that wild auburn hair that she kept tied back by a barrette or a rubber band.

The night of the accident, he'd wondered for a nanosecond if she was an angel. If she had been, he would have run to the light. Gladly.

After finishing his meal, he reached for the tub of low-fat chocolate ice cream and pulled off the circular cardboard top.

Before he could dig in, her voice sounded in the doorway. "Good evening."

John turned to his personal Florence Nightingale and smiled. "Hey. Come in."

He wasn't sure when he'd stopped thinking of her as a doctor. Pretty much the night he'd first laid eyes on her in the E.R., he guessed. He'd asked one of the nurses about her yesterday and had learned her name was Betsy. He'd also heard that she was one of the hardest working and most dedicated physicians on staff.

As she entered the room, she asked, "How's it going?"

"Fine." Did he dare tell her he was bored, that he wanted to get out of here, even if he didn't have any place to go?

When she reached his bedside, her petite frame hiding behind a pair of pale teal scrubs that made her eyes appear to be an even deeper shade of green, he studied her.

She wore very little makeup—not that she needed it—but she downplayed her beauty, which was a shame. He bet she'd look damn good in a sexy black dress with a low neckline, spiked high heels, her cheeks slightly flushed, a light coat of pink lipstick over lips that had a natural pout—a mouth he'd been paying a lot of attention to.

Her shoulder-length curls were pulled back into a simple ponytail, which was probably a logical style for a busy E.R. doctor. But John couldn't help imagining those locks hanging wild and free. Or envisioning her in an upscale jazz club, a lone saxophone playing a sultry tune in the background.

She placed her hand on the bedrail, her nails plain and neatly manicured. Her grip was light and tentative, though, as if she was a bit hesitant. A little nervous, even.

"I talked to Dr. Kelso," she said. "He's probably going to discharge you in the next day or so."

"He said something about that to me this morning. So I guess that means I'm almost back to fighting weight." John tried to toss her a carefree smile, but it probably fell short. He was as uneasy about the future as he was about the past, and it was a real stretch to pretend otherwise.

"Do you have any idea where you might like to go when you get out of here?" she asked.

If her gaze wasn't so damn sympathetic, if her eyes weren't so green, he might have popped off with something sarcastic. As it was, he shrugged. "Not yet. I keep hoping that I'll wake up and my memory will come rushing back. But it looks like I'd better give my options some thought."

"I have one for you," she said.

"An option?" He pushed the portable table aside, clearly interested. "What's that?"

"I talked to Dr. Graham. He needs some help on his ranch, if you don't mind doing some of the heavier chores for him. He's agreed to pay you a small salary and provide you with room and board. Of course, not until you're feeling up to it and Dr. Kelso has released you to go to work."

At the same ranch where Betsy lived? Had she gone to bat for him? It certainly seemed that way, and he could hardly wrap his mind around the fact that she'd done so for a stranger.

"Thanks for orchestrating things. I probably ought to stick around in Brighton Valley until... Well, until my life comes together for me again."

"It'll happen," she said. "Your memory will come back to you."

He wanted to believe her, but that's not exactly what Dr. Kelso had said. He'd used words like *probably* and *eventually*. But no one knew if or when John's memory would return. Or to what extent.

"For what it's worth," he told her with a grin, "things could change at any time. But for right now, you're the best friend I've got in the world."

*The best friend he had.*

The sincerity in John's words burrowed deep into Betsy's chest, pressing against her heart and stirring up all kinds of emotion—including a little guilt. Getting involved with her patients, even one she'd handed over to Jim Kelso, wasn't a good idea, especially when he was breathtakingly handsome.

So she tried to downplay his comment or thoughts about any kind of relationship with him. "I'm sure you have a lot of friends, family and acquaintances who would be here to visit you if they could."

"You might be right, but I'd be happy just to see my driver's license and to know my name." His gaze locked on hers, and she felt his frustration, his uneasiness.

She'd give anything to know more about him, too.

What kind of person was he? Honest and trustworthy? Loyal and caring?

Or was he a liar and a cheat?

She wished she could say that she had a sixth sense about that sort of thing, but she'd completely misread Doug, the man she'd once married.

They'd met at Baylor University, when he'd been a graduate student trying to earn an MBA and she'd been in medical school. She'd found him to be handsome and charming, the kind of man who could have had any woman on campus.

Looking back—and knowing what she did about his cheating nature—she realized he could have slept with the entire female student body and she never would have guessed.

She'd been naive back then, and if there were signs she should have picked up on, she'd missed seeing them. All she'd had to rely on were her feelings about him and her hormones. And boy, had *they* been wrong.

So how could she trust her instincts about John now, when she had even less to go on about him?

"A couple of police officers came by today," he

said, drawing her from her musing. "They asked about the robbery, but I couldn't provide them with any information."

She wished she could promise him that everything would come back to him someday, but there was a strong possibility that he wouldn't ever remember anything about the assault, just the things leading up to it and afterward.

"Were the officers able to give you any clues to your identity?" she asked.

"They told me that I'd had a little run-in at the bar with two local thugs who were harassing a cocktail waitress. They might have resented my interference and waited for me in the parking lot."

So John had a heroic nature? Betsy hoped that was the case. She'd hate to think she was drawn to another loser.

Time and again she'd promised herself she wouldn't let Doug's deceit completely shatter her ability to trust a man in the future. And each time her father showed a kindness to her ailing mother, each time he'd kissed her cheek or patted her frail knee, Betsy was reminded that good men did exist, that they honored their marriage vows. That they stuck by their women through sickness and health and through thick and thin.

But was John Doe one of them?

She couldn't be sure. And she feared falling for the wrong man again. That's why she'd focused on her medical practice after her divorce. And it's why she'd poured her heart and soul into her patients and the hospital.

After all, she had a skill and a responsibility to heal.

And she wasn't going to let anyone or anything interfere with her calling again.

But now here she was, visiting a man she knew nothing about, thinking about him in a purely feminine way. And while she'd tried to convince herself that her interest in him was influenced by a desire to see him heal and get on with his life, she knew better than that.

She was attracted to her patient.

Or rather, to *a* patient. John Doe was no longer *hers,* so she could easily nullify the rule, at least in her mind. But her attraction to him was increasing by leaps and bounds, and that was unsettling.

He reached over and tapped the top of her hand, which was resting on the bedrail. His fingertips lingered on her skin for only a second or two, but the heat of his touch sent her nerve endings helter-skelter, her blood racing.

"What's the matter?" he asked. "What's bothering you?"

"Nothing." She tried to smile, to shake it off. "Why do you ask?"

"Because you're wearing a pensive expression, one that tells me you're a thousand miles away."

"No, I'm still here." She forced her smile to deepen, her gaze to zero in on his.

He'd obviously picked up on the fact that she was distracted—but it wasn't because of another case or dilemma that worried her. It was clearly him causing her mind and thoughts to wander.

And she couldn't risk letting that happen. Whatever was going on between them had to be one-sided. And even if it wasn't, she couldn't stay at his bedside a moment longer. Not when her body was going whacky, just being around him.

So she glanced at her wristwatch, then back at him. "I have a meeting with a colleague before my shift starts, which means I need to go."

Honesty was always her policy, so even little white lies never sat easy with her. But she couldn't think of another excuse to leave.

"I'll see you tomorrow," he said, as if her visits had become a ritual they both could count on—and look forward to.

She wanted to remind him that it wasn't a done deal, but she'd already tossed out Doc's offer for him to stay on the ranch. And John had agreed.

So she stepped away from his bed. "Have a good evening."

"You, too."

As she turned and walked out of his room, she picked up her pace as though she could outrun all she'd been feeling back there, but reality dogged her down the corridor and into the elevator.

John had only touched her—and just briefly at that. But the fact that she'd reacted so strongly to something so minor left her unbalanced and skittish.

She did her best to regain control of her senses, but it wasn't easy.

When the elevator doors opened on the second floor and she stepped into the corridor that led to the cafeteria, she tried another tack.

Okay, so she was sexually attracted to John Doe. What was wrong with that? It's not as though she had to actually act upon that attraction.

And there was probably a very good reason for it, too—one that went beyond the man's looks and the intoxicating sound of his voice.

She'd sworn off men and sex ever since she'd told Doug to pack his things and move out of the house they'd shared when they'd been together. She'd been determined to focus on her career, on her patients. And she wouldn't let a relationship get in the way of that again.

But she was only human, with sexual needs and desires that had been dormant for too long. So it was just her hormones at play. Her body was merely reacting to its basic need for sex and zooming in on a possible candidate.

That's all it was.

She just needed a sexual release. But where did she find a potential partner, especially in Brighton Valley? And what about the hours she kept?

It was going to be tough. Especially when John Doe was the first sexual interest she'd had since she and Doug had split.

But there was no way she'd sleep with a patient. Especially one who had no idea where he'd come from or where he was going next.

Of course, with John Doe living only a couple of yards away from her house, she feared she was fighting a losing battle.

## Chapter Four

After her shift ended the next morning, Betsy once again took the elevator up to the third floor. But this time she was going to stop by John's room for practical reasons.

When she reached his doorway, she found him standing at the window, looking toward a copse of trees and scanning the hills that surrounded the medical center.

He was wearing a hospital gown, which was tied in back, and she couldn't help but smile. Those ugly, frumpy garments weren't the least bit flattering on patients, but the one he had on looked pretty darn good on him.

She had to admit that that was because his loose-fitting gown gaped open a bit, revealing a stretch of skin at the shoulder—and another near his butt.

As if sensing her presence, he turned and met her gaze.

"Good morning," she said. "It's nice to see you up and around."

He shot her a smile that nearly took her breath away. "I was just checking out the view."

She'd been doing the same thing, only not on the rolling hills and the stark bushes that had been full of colorful blooms a few months earlier.

He made his way back toward the bed, but instead of throwing back the blanket and climbing between the sheets, he took a seat in the chair next to it. "I'm really looking forward to getting out of here. I keep sensing that I have something to do, someplace to be."

She was sure that he did. But his other life had been temporarily denied him.

"That may be a good sign," she said.

"Me wanting to get out of here? Or feeling like I've dropped the ball?"

"Both. Your injuries are healing, and you're a healthy man. Lying around all day has got to be boring." She entered his room and took a seat at the edge of his bed. "You had a life prior to the accident. There must be a lot of things that need doing. And if you feel pressed about something, then one day soon it will all come back to you."

"I hope you're right."

She nodded at the built-in wardrobe where patients could keep their personal property. "Do you mind if I take a look in there?"

"Why?"

"Because the clothes you were wearing the other night are in there. And because they're dirty and bloody. I thought I'd wash them for you so you don't have to wear a hospital gown home—not that it doesn't look dashing."

He glanced down at his chest, then tugged at the cotton fabric. "I guess this isn't what all the ranch hands are wearing this year."

"No, I'm afraid you'd get a couple of laughs. Especially if you add a pair of cowboy boots to round out your ensemble."

A grin tugged at the side of his mouth, and his eyes glimmered. "Now that's a lousy visual."

"On you? I'd have to see it," she began, then reeled in her thoughts. What in the world was she doing? Flirting with him?

As much as she'd hoped to avoid John Doe for the rest of his stay in Brighton Valley, she had to face the facts. He'd been invited to stay at Doc's ranch, and he'd accepted.

He also had nowhere else to go.

So she crossed the room to the little closet and pulled open the door. A white plastic bag in which one of the nurses had packed the dirty clothes he'd been wearing sat next to a dusty pair of expensive Italian shoes.

Again, she was reminded that he hadn't been dressed like any of the men who called Brighton Valley home. He was going to need something suitable to wear on the ranch—jeans and boots for a starter.

Leaving the loafers behind, she removed the bag and shut the closet door.

"Can I look at those before you take them?" he asked.

"Of course." She carried the bag to him, then waited as he peered inside.

"Do they look familiar?" she asked.

He slowly shook his head and handed them back to her. "I wish they did."

Her heart went out to him, even though she wished it hadn't. And she felt herself being drawn closer to him, more involved.

"Then if it's all right with you," she said, "I'll take these home with me, wash them and bring them back this evening when I come to work."

"I hate to have you go to the trouble."

She offered him a smile. "Don't worry about it. You'll be carrying your own weight before you know it."

"You can count on *that.*"

He'd said it as if he meant it, and she believed him.

Or did she just want to believe that he was conscientious and responsible?

She lifted her wrist and checked her watch, even though there really wasn't any reason to. The motion had become a signal she used to make her excuses and leave, to let people know that she had a schedule to keep—whether she did or not.

"Well," she said, "I'd better go. I'll see you tonight."

"Thanks," he said. "I really appreciate all you've done. You've gone above and beyond for me, and you don't have to."

No, she didn't. And she probably *shouldn't.* But every time she gazed into his eyes, every time she spotted his vulnerability and sensed how lost he was, she couldn't seem to leave well enough alone.

"Just pay it forward," she said, letting him know there

weren't any strings attached, that she was just doing a good deed.

Then she left his room, took the elevator down to the lobby and headed to the parking lot. After climbing into her Honda Civic, she started the twenty-minute drive back to the ranch.

She had to give the poor guy credit. He'd been dealt a bad hand and was taking each day as it came. But for the time being, he didn't have anything but the clothes he'd been wearing on Wednesday night.

As she spotted a Wal-Mart sign up ahead, it dawned on her that John was going to need more than a single outfit and shoes. And without giving it much thought, she pulled into the driveway and parked near the front door.

Then she took a quick peek into the bag of dirty clothing. The pants, a top-designer brand, had a thirty-four-inch waist, and the shirt and jacket were both size large.

She had a feeling John wasn't the type to shop for clothes at a discount store, but this was the best she could do, the best she was *willing* to do. Her time was limited today, and she wasn't going to hang around town until one of the nicer clothing stores opened. She really needed to go home and get some rest before her next shift started.

Twenty minutes later, she returned to her car carrying several bags filled with things John would need—shaving cream, razors, a popular aftershave, a toothbrush and toothpaste. She also picked up socks, boxer shorts and Wranglers, as well as a couple of shirts and a rugged pair of boots that were on sale, something suitable for walking around the ranch.

Okay, so her credit card had taken a direct hit, but he couldn't very well get by without a change of clothes or toiletries.

By the time she arrived at the ranch, Doc was out in the yard waiting for her. But that didn't surprise her. The two had grown close over the years, and he thought of her as a daughter.

"You're late," he said, as he approached her car, clearly worried. "I was just getting ready to call and see what was keeping you. I was afraid you might have fallen asleep on the way home and run into a ditch."

"I'm all right, Doc."

A crisp morning breeze kicked up a hank of his white hair, and he crossed his arms. "You can tell everyone else that you're holding up just fine, but I know you've been burning the candle at both ends."

At one time, Dr. Graham had been the only physician in the valley, and Betsy wasn't doing anything he hadn't done every day of his fifty-year practice.

"The night shifts are tough," she admitted, as she pulled the blue plastic bags from her car. "But I've got a day off tomorrow. I can catch up on my sleep then."

"What'd you do?" he asked, nodding to the bags she held. "Go shopping on the way home?"

"I picked up a few things for John Doe. All he has are the clothes he was wearing."

Her friend and mentor grimaced. "You didn't need to spend any money. I've got plenty of old clothes he can wear. In fact, I've already gathered them together and have them ready for him."

"But they might not be the right size." And even if John could make do with an elderly man's hand-me-downs, she doubted that the younger man would like wearing them. Doc may have been dapper in his day, but his sense of style was probably a little old-fashioned or bucolic for a man like John.

*A man like John.*

And just what kind of man was that? The irony struck her hard, and she let out a weary sigh.

Still, she carried her purchases, as well as John's laundry, into Doc's house.

"Do you mind if I use your washing machine?" she asked.

"Of course not." He followed her to the service porch, where he kept his washer and dryer.

He watched as she set aside her purchases, then opened the white plastic bag and dumped out the dirty clothing onto the worktable next to the appliances.

As she separated the dark slacks from the white shirt, shorts and socks, she asked, "Do you have any colors I can put in with his pants?"

"Yes, but just leave those things right there. You're getting those dark circles under your eyes again and you need to get some rest. I'll take care of that for you."

"All right." She lifted the lid to the washer and dropped the slacks inside. Then she leaned forward, went up on tiptoe and brushed a kiss on Doc's wrinkled cheek. "What would I do without you?"

"Run yourself into the ground, I suspect."

She smiled and gave him a hug. "Thanks, Doc. Then I'll just take this other stuff into the spare bedroom and lay them out for him. After that, I'll go home, take a hot shower and fix a cup of chamomile tea. I'll probably be asleep before you know it."

She gathered the Wal-Mart bags, and as she headed for the guest room, Doc tagged along behind her.

"I wish you wouldn't have spent your hard-earned money on that fellow," her friend said. "He's probably going to leave town within the next couple of days and take all the new things with him."

Doc had a point, but this was the holiday season, a time of goodwill and glad tidings. "The expense won't break me. Besides, you remember what the Good Book says, 'It's more blessed to give than receive.'"

As she laid out the shaving gear and toiletries she'd purchased, Doc left the room and returned with a stack of clothes. "These pants used to fit me before I had that gall-bladder surgery last spring. If they're too big around the waist, he can use a belt to cinch 'em up. And he can cuff them if they're too long."

"I'm sure he'll appreciate the gesture."

At least, she hoped he would. There was so much about the man she didn't know....

"This is just a temporary fix," Doc said. "I'm sure his memory will eventually return, and when it does, he'll head back to wherever he came from."

That was true. John Doe was just passing through her life—here today and gone tomorrow.

And whether she'd be happy about that or not was left to be seen.

Dr. Kelso discharged John on Friday, which worked out well since Betsy was off that day and could drive out to the hospital to pick him up.

When she entered his room, she found him dressed in the outfit he'd been wearing when he'd arrived at the Stagecoach Inn last Wednesday night, the one that Doc had laundered and she'd pressed for him. Black slacks, a white shirt and expensive leather shoes.

"It looks like you're ready to go," she said.

"I'm waiting for someone to bring a wheelchair, which seems crazy to me. I can walk."

"It's hospital policy."

"That's what the nurse said."

For an awkward moment, silence stretched between them, and while she probably ought to make small talk to break the tension, she sketched a gaze over him.

Just as she'd suspected, he stood over six feet tall, with dark hair that curled up at his collar and eyes that could soften the hardest of hearts. He looked sharp and stylish, and she could easily imagine the impression he'd left on the rednecks and cowboys who'd been at the honky-tonk last Wednesday night.

Witnesses had said that he'd left the bar alone. And if that were the case, then he'd done so by choice. Any woman on the prowl—married or single—would have jumped at the chance to go home with him.

Maybe he hadn't been interested in romance.

And if not, she wondered why. Was he already committed to someone?

The moment the question crossed her mind, she realized she was trying too hard to read into things. His memory would eventually return, and when it did, she'd have the answers she needed.

Or, at least, he would.

Shrugging off her curiosity the best she could, she said, "I'm sure the wheelchair is on its way."

"I hope so. I'm also going to have to stop by the accounting office, but that won't take long."

She supposed it wouldn't because he didn't have the means to pay the bill. But neither of them broached that fact.

"Maybe they can put me on some kind of payment plan," he said. "It's also possible that I have health insurance and the details will come to me later. Either way, I'll make it right."

She hoped he meant that for several reasons. First of all, the hospital was already struggling to make ends meet, and they didn't need one more financial burden. And second, she wanted to believe that integrity came natural to him.

He certainly seemed convincing, but that was left to be seen. So far, the only things Betsy knew about John were guesswork and hunches.

And given her track record, who knew how accurate those would prove to be?

"Tell you what," she said. "I'll get my car and pull it up to the curb in front of the hospital. You can find me when you're done in the office."

He nodded, and she left his room, eager to escape all the what-ifs that seemed to crop up whenever she was around him.

Minutes later, she sat in her idling car outside the lobby entrance to the medical center, waiting for someone to bring John out to the curb. But she didn't have to wait long. The automatic door soon swung open, and

Stan Thompson, one of the hospital volunteers, pushed John's wheelchair outside.

Betsy waved, letting the men know that she was in the white Civic. And when John smiled in return, her heart spun in her chest.

She hoped it wasn't a big mistake to take him to Doc's ranch. But the plan had already been set in motion, and there wasn't much she could do about it now.

As John climbed from the chair and slid into the passenger seat of her car, they both thanked Stan, and then they were on their way.

"It was nice of Dr. Graham to let me stay with him," John said, breaking the silence.

"He's a great guy. And he's got a heart as big as they make them."

"Apparently so." John peered out the passenger window at the passing scenery, the cattle in the fields, the pale green water tower with the name *Brighton Valley* painted across it in bold black letters.

She'd studied the same sights when she'd first come to town, and she wondered if he liked what he saw, if he felt as though he'd come home, too.

"It's peaceful out here," he finally said.

"I think so." It was one reason she liked living outside of town and didn't mind the extra time it took to drive to work.

"How far is the ranch from here?" he asked.

"About twenty minutes."

"Is it a bad commute?"

There it went again—another hunch based upon something as simple as a word choice. Did John live in a large city? One in which people talked about their commutes to work?

Rather than continue to make those kinds of leaps, she answered his question. "No, it's not bad. Although I do wish I lived a little closer to town. My parents live at the Shady Glen Retirement Home, so it would mean a lot less driving time."

"Are your parents elderly?" he asked.

She nodded. "My mom and dad were married for twenty years before they adopted me."

"Are you an only child?"

"Yes."

John stared out the windshield, watching the road ahead. He seemed to ponder her statement for a while, then he turned to her and added, "They must be very proud of you."

"They are." She thought about her mom and dad, about how they'd cheered each of her successes, how they'd shared all they had with her. A warm smile stretched across her face. "I'm proud of them, too."

"Oh, yeah? Why's that?"

"Because they fell in love and made a lifetime commitment to each other. A lot of people aren't that lucky— or that dedicated to each other. I certainly wasn't."

"So you're divorced?"

She hadn't meant to share any personal details with him, especially about Doug and their split, but it was a little late to backpedal now. John had already picked up on it. "Yes, I was married right after I got out of med school. But it didn't work out."

"Why? Because you weren't lucky or dedicated?"

"*I* wasn't lucky, and *he* wasn't dedicated."

He let it go for a moment, as if trying to make sense of what she'd said—and what she hadn't. Then he asked, "So how did luck play into it?"

"I think people who meet the perfect partner and fall in love are incredibly fortunate." She shrugged. "And I wasn't."

"I take it your ex wasn't in it for the long haul," John said, filling in the blanks.

He might have been an attorney or a police detective in his real life. Or else he was good at probing for answers.

If anyone else had been quizzing her, she might have considered them rude. But for some reason, she didn't think John was overstepping his bounds. He knew so little about himself that a conversation like this might trigger his own memories.

"All the time I spent at the hospital took a toll on our relationship," she said, still holding back.

She could have told him that Doug had cheated, but there was a part of her that didn't want to admit that her love hadn't been enough for him.

"Does he—your ex-husband—live around here?"

"He's from Houston. When we split, I wanted to put some distance between us. That's when I bought Doc's practice and moved to Brighton Valley."

"And your parents came with you?"

"I couldn't imagine my life without them or not being able to visit them at a moment's notice. On top of that, my mom's having a few health issues, and I can monitor them easier if she's nearby."

"I'm sorry. Are those 'issues' serious?"

"They could be, but medication is helping. And she's got a great outlook on life."

"Even living in a rest home?"

"Shady Glen isn't a convalescent hospital. The residents are all free to come and go as they please. And my parents are pretty active. In fact, they left yesterday on a trip to Galveston with some of the other residents." Betsy let the subject ride for a couple of minutes, then glanced across the seat at her passenger, a handsome stranger who now knew a lot more information about her than he did about himself.

Before he could comment or quiz her any further, she added, "And for what it's worth, I'd planned to buy a house in town and have them live with me, but they insisted upon moving into Shady Glen. It's worked out well, though. And it was the right decision for them to make. They've been able to maintain their independence while living in a safe environment, which is important. And they've made friends with their neighbors."

"That's great."

She let his words and the subject trail off, as she focused on the road ahead. She wasn't going to share any more intimate details with John, even if there seemed to be a friendship brewing between them.

But they couldn't possibly become friends—or anything else. Not until she learned more about him.

As the car neared the county road that would take them to Doc's ranch, she tossed another casual glance John's way, only to find him looking at her, too.

Their gazes locked, holding her with some kind of invisible grip, and she realized her resolve to keep an emotional distance wasn't holding up.

And even if his identity and his past were still a mystery, she'd certainly settle for knowing what was going on in his mind.

Was she the only one feeling a sexual charge whenever their eyes met?

John tore his gaze away from Betsy's and tried to get his thoughts on an even keel.

He had no business getting involved with anyone until his memory returned. Trouble was, there was something about the beautiful E.R. doctor that made it impossible for him to keep his distance.

Sure, there'd been an instant attraction, which wasn't surprising. She was a beautiful woman—bright, successful and caring. And she was the only person in this world who seemed to have his back.

But damn. His attraction was growing by leaps and bounds. And he couldn't believe that he was the only one feeling it.

After all, she must have set up the deal between him and Doc Graham, a man who'd never even met him.

As they neared the ranch, John found himself studying the grassy pastures, the grazing cattle and an occasional windmill. None of it looked familiar, yet it brought on a strange sense of comfort, as if he was really going home and not just to a temporary job and place to sleep while he was stuck in Brighton Valley.

Either way, he had a feeling that this might be just what the doctor ordered.

And speaking of doctors…

He stole another peek at Betsy, who was wearing a pair of black jeans and a cream-colored sweater today.

Her hair was still held back in a clip in her usual businesslike manner. But she was prettier than she'd been in the hospital, more approachable and down-to-earth. She'd put on some lipstick and mascara, and he wondered if she'd done it for him.

"Here it is," she said as she drove down a narrow but paved road to a pale blue clapboard house with a veranda-style front porch, an old barn and several outbuildings.

"Which one is the guesthouse?" he asked.

She pointed toward a grassy knoll, where a white stucco building sat off by itself. It had a pale green door and was adorned with matching window boxes. "Doc built it for his wife's sister about ten years ago. She'd just lost her husband and had a heart condition. But she died before she was able to move in."

"Doc must be a generous and kindhearted man."

"He's the best."

As they got out of the car, an elderly man with a head of thick white hair stood up from where he'd been seated on the porch and started toward them.

John met him halfway and extended his hand. "I want you to know how much I appreciate your offer to let me stay here. Dr. Kelso said I've got to take it easy for another week or so, but as soon as I'm able, I'll do whatever I can to help you out."

Dr. Graham took his hand and gave it a gentleman's shake. "It'll be a win-win for both of us. Come on. I'll show you to your room."

John looked at Betsy. "Are you coming, too?"

She didn't answer right away, and he wondered if she

was going to make up some excuse and bow out. But instead, she smiled. "Sure. Why not?"

Why not, indeed.

Betsy Nielson intrigued him more each time he saw her, each time he talked to her and she uncovered another layer of her past. Too bad it wasn't his past that was unfolding, but he couldn't stew about that now. He was stuck in Brighton Valley and had to make the best of it.

There was an upside, though. A powerful attraction appeared to be brewing between the two of them.

And if a romance developed?

He'd be hard-pressed to try to stop it.

## Chapter Five

John was surprised to see that Betsy had picked up some of the toiletries he would need, as well as boxer shorts, socks and a couple of outfits.

"I don't know what to say." He studied the clothing purchases, which had been laid out on the double bed in Doc's guest room. Then he caught her eye and smiled. "Thanks for doing this for me."

"You're welcome."

She turned away, as if the intimacy made her uneasy, and pointed to the shaving gear and toiletries she'd placed on the bureau. "If you need anything else, let me know. I can pick it up for you the next time I'm in town."

"This ought to do it. Thanks again."

She nodded, then left the room.

John might have forgotten a lot of things, like his name and occupation, but he somehow knew that people weren't always that kind to strangers. And that Betsy was showing her true character, that she was more than a pretty face and a skilled physician.

Thanks to Dr. Graham's prodding, she stayed long enough to join them for lunch, a simple fare of grilled cheese sandwiches, chips and fruit. They made small talk while they ate, then she excused herself and went home.

John was sorry to see her go, although he knew she needed some rest. It might be her day off, but working nights had to be rough. He figured she could stand to catch a little shut-eye whenever she had a chance.

A nap wouldn't hurt him, either. He might be feeling better and getting stronger each day, but his body was still recuperating from the beating and he didn't want to push it. Not when he needed his brain to heal as quickly as possible. He was eager to get on with his life—wherever that might be.

After Betsy left, Doc said he was going to sit on the porch and read a bit.

"Do you want to join me?" he asked. "I've got a good-size collection of books you can choose from in my den."

"Maybe later, thanks. I think I'd rather lie down for a while. It's been a few days since I've gotten this active."

John followed Doc into the living room, where the old man stopped by the lamp table closest to an easy chair and picked up a hardbound Dean Koontz novel.

Before slipping off to the bedroom John had been given, he scanned the cozy living area, noting the stone fireplace and hand-carved mantel, where several framed photographs were displayed.

Figuring Doc had meant for his guests to check out the photos of his friends and family, John eased closer to the mantel and took a look at them.

There was a black-and-white snapshot of a young Dr. Graham wearing a military uniform and standing next to an attractive blonde. John assumed the woman was his wife, and as he found an older picture of the couple near the Eiffel Tower, he decided his assumption was correct.

There was a photograph of Betsy with a smiling gray-haired couple seated by a decorated Christmas tree. John guessed they were with her parents, even though he didn't notice a resemblance. Then he remembered that she was adopted, so that would explain it.

He wondered if she'd ever looked for her biological family. Some people felt compelled to do that. And if she were one of them, then maybe that's why she'd taken him under her wing. She understood how lost he felt without having a sense of his roots.

As he thought of Betsy and their commonalities, he glanced at the door she'd walked out of earlier, wishing she was still here.

But there was no need to stew about that. So he replaced the frame on the mantel, then walked to the hallway that led to the bedrooms.

As he slipped into the privacy of his room, which was simply decorated with a dresser and a double bed, his eye was drawn to a picture hanging on the wall. It was just a print of two curly-haired cherubs, nothing remarkable or expensive. He'd glossed over it before, yet he was drawn to it now.

It looked oddly familiar, as if he'd seen it before.

For a moment, a vision flashed before him of a silver-haired woman wearing a floral-print apron and a warm smile.

The scent of tomatoes, cilantro and spice.

Children's laughter.

The sound of a screen door slamming.

But the wisp of a memory faded before he could wrap his mind around it, leaving him grasping for mental straws.

What did it mean? Was his life coming back to him?

God, he sure hoped so.

As if he could hurry it along, he kicked off his shoes and climbed on top of the bed, which was covered with a calico quilt. The old-fashioned box springs squeaked from his weight as he settled into the comfort of the mattress.

He closed his eyes and tried to recall the disjointed recollection—the sight, the scents and the sounds that had disappeared as quickly as they'd formed. But the vague memory was lost to him, along with his past.

The clock on the dresser ticktocked, lulling him to sleep. He awoke hours later to the sound of a knock at his door and the aroma of chicken baking in the oven.

"Dinner's ready," Doc said.

"I'll be right there." John climbed out of bed, straightened the quilt he'd been laying on and the pillow he'd been using. Then he went into the bathroom and washed his face and hands.

When he finished, he joined Doc at the kitchen table. "It sure smells good."

"Doesn't it? It's a chicken-and-rice casserole. Betsy came by earlier and put it in the oven for us."

"Does she cook for you often?"

"Whenever she gets the chance. She thinks I need someone to fuss over me."

"And you don't agree?"

"Who doesn't like a little TLC?" the old man said with a wink.

John agreed, especially if Betsy was the one providing it. "Is she going to eat with us?"

"No, not this evening."

John wondered why, but he didn't ask. There wasn't any need for Dr. Graham to think he was hoping for a little tender loving care himself. Or for him to think John was crushing on the pretty redhead who lived only a few footsteps away.

While they ate, Doc chatted about his life as the only physician in the valley, about some of the miracles and mishaps he'd been a witness to.

John found the man and his stories more than a little interesting, and each time Doc grew quiet, John asked him a question, just as he'd done with Betsy earlier. He'd spent too many lonely days in the hospital with only the television to keep him company. And because he had nothing to offer in terms of his own past, he enjoyed getting to know the new people in his life.

Of course, the one he wanted to know the most about was Betsy.

"Why doesn't she work days? Is she a night owl by nature?"

"Actually, she's a real team player and steps in whenever the hospital is shorthanded. And that means she's got the worst of both worlds. Sometimes she works nights, then she's back on days. And changing shifts like that is really tough."

"Sounds like she's a good employee."

"And loyal to a fault," Doc said as he stood and began to gather the empty plates.

John scooted his chair back and got to his feet. "Let me help."

"Nope," Doc said, "not tonight. You need to take it easy for the next day or two. And then, at that point, I'll let you start doing some of the easier chores. We'll slowly build up from there."

John wouldn't argue with the man because this was his first day out of the hospital. But he wasn't ready for bed, either. So he asked, "Do you mind if I sit out on the porch for a while?"

"Not at all," the old man said. "It's not too cold tonight, but you might want a jacket. I've got one hanging on the coat tree in the living room. Help yourself."

"Thanks."

John made his way to the front of the house. Then he took the black corduroy jacket from the hook, slipped it on and went out on the porch where two wicker rockers sat.

Once outside in the winter evening, he couldn't help wishing that the crisp air would clear his mind. He'd been disappointed that no one in the medical field had been able to tell him when his memory would return, but the brief vision he'd had earlier today suggested it was coming—one piece at a time.

He took a seat in one of the rockers and tried to find comfort in the beautiful winter night. But all he could seem to think about was how insignificant he and his amnesia were in the scheme of things.

As he glanced at the empty chair beside him, he wondered if Doc ever sat out here with Betsy.

Just the thought of the attractive woman caused him to seek out her house, to notice the lamp on inside her living-room window. Did that mean she was awake?

And if so, would she like company?

What would she think if he showed up unannounced?

The idea was still in the thinking stage when her porch light went on, her front door swung open and she stepped outside.

He watched as she made her way across the yard and approached Doc's house.

Did she know John was out here? Would his presence startle her?

"Hey," he said, wanting to let her know he was on the porch. "What are you doing?"

"Just coming over to check on Doc. What's he up to this evening?"

"Reading, I suspect. He's really gotten into that novel."

She continued to approach the porch, as if Doc wasn't the only one she'd come to see about. And it pleased him to think that she cared about how he was faring.

"It's a nice night," he said. "Are you up for some stargazing?"

"Sure." She took a seat in the rocker next to his and set hers into motion, the chair squeaking and creaking against the wood flooring.

They didn't talk right away, didn't really need to. The evening sky, with its nearly full moon and massive splatter of twinkling stars, was providing them with an amazing celestial display.

John easily found the Big and Little Dippers, as well as Polaris, which had played a big role in helping the people traveling on the underground railroad. In fact, there'd been a coded song called "Follow the Drinking Gourd" that had helped the escaped slaves find their way to freedom in the north.

How weird was that? he wondered. The basic knowledge he'd accrued over the years didn't seem to be affected by his amnesia, yet he couldn't remember the people, the places or the things that had been a part of his life before he'd set foot in Brighton Valley.

As he pondered the injustice of it all, Betsy said, "The stars are prettier than usual tonight."

"I was thinking the same thing. Being out in the country like this makes a big difference. You don't get the full effect of the night sky in the city."

She turned to him. "That's the second thing you've said to lead me to believe that you're a city boy."

He considered her comment, but other than the words that had slipped out of his mouth, he couldn't say one way or the other. So he shrugged. "I'm not sure where that came from."

"So you're still drawing a blank?"

"Pretty much. I do know that I drink my coffee black and I'm not too fond of vegetables."

"The rest will come."

He didn't see any reason to agree or to argue, so he let it go and stole a look at his pretty companion as she sat in the rocker, her hands perched on the armrests.

She was seated close enough to touch, close enough for him to take hold of her hand and give it a warm and gentle squeeze. But he knew better than to overstep his boundaries, no matter how much he'd like to. So instead of boldly touching her, he continued to take in the starlit sky and the smell of night-blooming jasmine, the sounds of a cow lowing in the distance.

He wasn't sure how long they'd sat here, together in pensive silence and appreciation.

A few minutes, he supposed.

When he turned to offer her a smile, he saw that her eyes were closed and her head was resting against the back of the chair.

Hadn't she gotten any rest this afternoon? He had a feeling that she hadn't. No wonder Doc had been worried about her.

He let her rest for a while longer, then decided to wake her so she could go to bed, where she'd be more comfortable. So he reached over and placed his hand over hers, felt the softness of her skin, the warmth.

While he knew he should give her hand a little nudge and jar her awake, he held back for a moment and basked in the intimacy of their touch, in the connection they shared for one moment in time.

In a way, it made him feel less alone. Less isolated. Less cornered into a reality that wasn't of his own making.

Finally, he stroked the top her hand, his fingers sliding over her knuckles. "Betsy?"

Her eyes fluttered opened and she turned to face him. "Yes?"

With reluctance, he withdrew his hand. "It's time for bed."

She blinked several times and yawned. Then she slowly got to her feet. "I'm sorry for dozing off."

"Don't be. But I hope you're going to start working the day shift soon."

"I'm off this weekend." She shoved her hands in the pockets of her knit jacket. "And on Monday, I'm back to working days until the medical center needs me again."

"Good. I'm not sure how healthy it is for you to be bouncing back and forth between shifts."

She smiled. "Have you been talking to Doc? He's been worried about me, but I know when to slow down and when to take it easy."

John hoped so and tossed her an I'm-glad-to-hear-it smile.

"I'll see you tomorrow," she said, as she started down the steps and headed for the guesthouse.

As she left him on the porch, he rubbed his thumb over his fingertips, which were still warm and charged from their brief physical contact.

Touching Betsy had been much nicer than he'd expected it to be. And for a moment, in spite of the vastness of the sky and the innumerable celestial lights shining throughout the universe, he didn't feel the least bit insignificant.

* * *

For the next five days, John didn't get to see nearly as much of Betsy as he would have liked. Her work schedule hadn't allowed for more than a few occasional visits, which was too bad.

But on the bright side, he'd started doing more around the ranch to help Dr. Graham and to pay for his keep. He still didn't know much about the man he used to be, but it appeared that hard work came naturally to him.

And so did being around horses.

Apparently, he had some experience working on a ranch and seemed to know things without being told, which led him to believe he'd done his share of mucking stalls and grooming horses in the past.

And something told him that he'd liked it.

There was a palomino mare with a sweet disposition who'd taken to him, but it was a spirited roan gelding that had really caught his eye.

"Do you think it would be okay if I took him for a ride one of these days?" he'd asked Doc over dinner.

"Sure, as long as you don't do anything foolish, like running or jumping. You're not ready for anything that strenuous yet."

"I'll be careful. No one wants to see me get better more than I do."

"You're right. And for what it's worth, it's been nice having your company, son. So don't think I'm in any hurry to see you leave. There aren't too many young people who have time for a rambling old man."

John chuckled. "You'll have to introduce me to him. I haven't met any rambling old men around here."

Dr. Graham, with his thick head of white hair, lively

blue eyes and quick wit, could put an interesting spin on a conversation, and John couldn't help but like him.

"And speaking of having you around," Doc said as he got to his feet, "let's get these dishes done."

"You got it."

There wasn't much to clean up this evening, but John helped by putting the leftovers into the fridge and wiping the counters, while Doc filled the dishwasher. Then, as was becoming their habit in the evenings, Doc picked up his novel—this time one by Michael Crichton—and settled into his easy chair, while John went out to the porch.

But it wasn't fresh air or peace and quiet that he was seeking; it was Betsy. She'd been working the day shift this past week and usually got home around eight. But it was well past that now.

He lifted his wrist to check the time, a useless habit that continued after his mugging. And as he glanced at the place where a watch used to be, he was again reminded of all that had been stolen from him.

It had to be close to nine when Betsy finally arrived home, and John got up from his seat and met her in the driveway.

"I was getting worried about you," he said, as he approached her car.

"My parents just got home from their trip to Galveston this afternoon, so I stopped by to see them."

"Did they have fun?"

"Well, the bus broke down once. But other than that, they had a great time." Betsy pushed the remote on her key chain, locking the doors. "My mom picked up a boysenberry-flavored herb tea while she was gone, so I stayed and had a cup with her."

They walked to the porch, but she didn't take a seat. Instead, she stood at the railing and peered into the Texas night. There was something about this place that renewed her spirit and cleared her head.

"It's nice that you and your parents are close," John said.

Betsy smiled and turned away from the railing, facing John instead. "I've really been blessed."

"Have you ever wanted to find your biological parents?"

The question took her aback, but she answered truthfully. "No, not really."

She'd always been curious about her birth parents, of course, but she'd never tried to track them down. She wouldn't do anything that might hurt the people who'd raised her and had earned the titles of Mom and Dad. So she'd embraced the wonderful parents she had.

"Don't you ever wonder about them?"

"Sure. I think most people who've been adopted do." She studied the man before her, realizing he knew less about his birth family than she did. And she found herself telling him something she hadn't told anyone else. "Actually, my biological mother's attorney contacted me a couple of weeks ago and asked to set up a meeting."

"And did you? Agree to meet her?"

"Not right now."

She couldn't deny a curiosity about the woman, especially after the attorney had said, "She'd like to know if your hair is still red. It was that color when you were a newborn."

Many women who gave up their babies chose not to see them or hold them, and Betsy wondered if her birth mom had been an exception. A part of her hoped so.

Nevertheless, she told the woman's attorney that yes, she was a redhead. And that her life was a little too complicated to set up a meeting for the time being.

Besides, getting involved in any kind of relationship right now, especially with a woman she knew nothing about, could really complicate her life.

It would be risky, too. What if she was disappointed? What if she met her biological family and realized they could have made television appearances on *The Jerry Springer Show?*

No, she didn't want to deal with anything like that now. And even if she did, there was one thing she valued above everything else: people who'd proven themselves as loving, dependable and trustworthy.

"In some ways, we've got a lot in common," he said. "Neither of us have much knowledge of our roots."

Yes, but while he'd probably give anything to learn more about his, she wasn't eager to face the changes that the past might make in her life. Not if it might hurt her parents.

He grew pensive for a moment, and she figured that he was wondering about his family, about the place he'd come from, and her heart went out to him.

As he glanced down at his feet, she took the time to study him. He was dressed in one of the new outfits she'd purchased—jeans and a flannel shirt. And he was wearing Doc's jacket again. He looked like any of the local ranchers, albeit a lot more handsome. Yet she had to remind herself that he was a stranger, no matter how familiar he seemed.

"So how did your day go?" she asked, trying to draw him from the thoughts that appeared to be dragging him down.

He looked up and shrugged. "I managed to get some work done. I repaired a gate on the corral and mucked out the stalls. Then I made friends with a couple of horses."

She couldn't help but laugh. "I've got to get you out into the real world and around more people."

"I don't know about that," he said. "Buck and Sadie are awfully nice. And they pretty much go along with everything I say."

"There's something to be said about that, I suppose."

Their gazes locked, and the humorous moment passed, leaving something else in its wake. Something charged with heat.

"Would you like to go riding with me someday?" he asked.

Was he thinking that the outing would be a date?

The spark in his eyes and a spike in her heart rate suggested that he was. Yet in spite of all the reasons she should decline, she couldn't help thinking a ride on a Sunday afternoon would be a nice change to her routine.

"Sure," she said, "but you'll have to give me a gentle horse. I'm really not what you'd call a cowgirl."

"It's pretty easy. I'll teach you whatever you need to know."

"You've got experience with horses?"

"I think so." His brow furrowed as he gave it some further thought.

So the man she'd considered a city boy had country roots? Or was she wrong about her assumptions?

She could see the same questions in his eyes, the frustration at not even knowing a few of the basics.

Unable to help herself, she reached out and stroked his cheek, fingering his solid, square-cut jaw, the faint bristle of his beard.

His gaze locked on hers, stirring up something deep within her, and any reservations about getting involved with him flew out the window.

As he lowered his mouth to hers, his musky, masculine scent assaulted her better judgment and set her mind swirling in a maelstrom of desire.

This was so not what she'd planned, but it no longer seemed to matter.

He brushed his lips against hers, once, twice, a third time. Then he took her mouth and claimed it as his own.

The kiss intensified, and she opened her mouth, letting his tongue mate with hers. She leaned into him, wrapping her arms around him, holding him close.

Closing her eyes, she let herself go, losing herself in a surge of pheromones and need, kissing him deeply, thoroughly.

She couldn't remember the last time she and Doug had kissed—certainly long before their split. But she couldn't remember it being anything like this. She tried to blame it on hormones and the sexual drought she'd been living in since her divorce. But something told her it had nothing to do with biology and everything to do with the man whose hands were exploring her back, her hips, her...

Oh, Lordy. Her knees were giving out on her, and an ache was settling deep in her core, demanding she throw caution to the wind. But Doug's deception was still too fresh on her mind, and so was her decision not to get involved with a stranger.

So she placed her hand on John's chest, where his heart pounded in a primal rhythm, announcing that the kiss had touched him in the same reckless way that it had her.

But someone had to be strong, had to consider the repercussions. And as she gave a gentle push against him, as she pulled her mouth from his, she grieved for what she was denying them.

He sucked in a breath and raked a hand through his hair, as though taken aback by the heat of what they'd just shared.

"I'm sorry," she said.

"Don't be."

It had only been a kiss, a small voice inside her argued. But it had been so much more than a kiss. It had been a sexual prelude to something she could only imagine.

"I shouldn't have let that happen," she said. "I don't want you to get the wrong idea."

"The wrong idea about what? The fact that we're attracted to each other? That kissing you again could lead to a whole lot more?"

All she had left was her honesty. "It was good to say the least. But a physical relationship isn't a good idea for either one of us at this point in time."

She'd already made one mistake in her life: she'd fallen for a man who wasn't the person she'd thought he was. And she was on the verge of repeating the same mistake.

If she hadn't already.

## Chapter Six

Betsy was in trouble.

*Big trouble.*

With her mind spinning, her senses reeling and her knees struggling to keep her body upright, she left John on the porch of Doc's house and returned home, determined to put the kiss they'd shared behind her. But she couldn't seem to get it out of her mind.

Had another man's kiss ever rocked her to the core like John's had? If so, she couldn't remember who the accomplished kisser could have been.

Certainly not Doug.

Once she let herself into the privacy of her cozy living room, she tried all of her old tricks for relaxing—a warm bubble bath and a cup of chamomile tea—but she didn't sleep a wink that night.

She finally picked up a book she'd been meaning to read, something she'd borrowed from Doc a few weeks ago and had set on her nightstand. But the opening pages of the mystery couldn't compete with the memory that still simmered in her mind, and she couldn't seem to lose herself in a fictional story. Not when she was so caught up in the reality of what had just happened.

By the time dawn broke over the ranch, she finally dozed off for a couple of hours. But she was up again by nine and decided to take a shower and start her day.

As she looked into the bathroom mirror, she saw those dark crescents under her eyes that Doc always managed to spot. She'd have to use makeup today or risk having him say something again.

All she needed was for Doc—or worse, *John*—to realize that she'd hardly slept a wink last night and to assume the kiss had anything to do with it. Trouble was, it had knocked her world off its axis. And she didn't want anyone to suspect that she was the least bit unbalanced by it.

So she showered and shampooed her hair. After drying off, she dressed quickly, choosing a pair of comfortable blue jeans and a green sweater. Next she applied a light coat of foundation, taking care to conceal the circles under her eyes, and topped it off with a bit of lipstick and mascara. Then she blow-dried her hair.

She didn't take time to do anything to it, other than pull it back in a rubber band. She had to get out of here. There was no way she could hang out at the ranch today and risk running into John.

What would she say to him? How would she act?

Sure, she'd told him last night that a relationship between them wasn't going anywhere. And it *wasn't*. She couldn't allow anything like that to happen until she knew more about him, about the values and personal ethics that drove him.

And whether he had a family waiting for him somewhere.

So, eager to disappear for the day, she called her parents and asked if they wanted to get a bite to eat.

"We play with our bridge group at two," her dad said. "But we'd love to have an early lunch with you, honey. What time will you be here?"

She glanced at her wristwatch. "About ten-thirty. We can decide where to go when I get there."

After ending the call, she grabbed her purse and walked out of the house, planning to make a beeline to her car. But once outside, she spotted Doc's red Chevy S-10 pickup with its hood raised.

John stood in front of the vehicle, peering at the engine as if checking the oil or fixing a loose wire.

As much as she'd like to blend into the ranch scenery and fade into the distance, she knew he would notice her and that she'd have to acknowledge him somehow.

And she'd been right. Just as she reached her car, John slammed down the hood and brushed his hands together.

Okay, she thought, it was showtime.

The minute he spotted her, a smile broke across his face, giving him a bright-eyed, bushy-tailed appearance. It seemed pretty safe to assume that thoughts of the kiss hadn't interrupted his sleep habits in the least.

"Good morning," she said, trying to appear cheerful and unaffected by the sight of him, even though her heart was doing loop de loops.

Her steps slowed as she watched him approach, the

late-morning sun glistening off the black strands of his hair, his blue eyes glimmering.

"Are you going someplace?" he asked.

She fingered the narrow shoulder strap of her purse. "Into town to see my folks. Why?"

"I have an appointment with Dr. Kelso at ten-thirty, and Doc said I could use his truck. But it won't start. It's turning over, so it's not the battery. I have a feeling it's going to need a new starter, but I don't have time to work on it now."

Was he a mechanic? Or did most men have an innate understanding of engines and motors?

She hated not knowing which it was in his case. And even worse, she hated the fact that she was always making assumptions about him, any or all of which could be way off base.

"I don't suppose I could catch a ride with you?" he said.

Jim Kelso's office was just a block or so down the street from Shady Glen, so it wouldn't be out of her way to drop him off.

Besides, what did she expect him to do? Call a cab or hitchhike?

"Sure," she said. "I can take you."

"That's great. Just give me a chance to tell Doc where I'm going."

Minutes later, John was back and climbing into the passenger seat of her Honda Civic. When he shut the door, filling the air in her lungs with the hint of soap, musk and man, the sides of the compact car seemed to close in on them, forcing them closer together.

As her heart rate soared in reaction to the sight, sound

and smell of him, she reminded herself to downplay her interest in him.

But as she turned the car around and headed down the driveway toward the road that led to Brighton Valley, she realized that pretending that she wasn't attracted to John Doe was going to be as easy as ignoring a full-grown elephant riding in the passenger seat of a compact car.

On the way to town, Betsy had been unusually quiet. She could be pondering a perplexing medical case or something work-related, John supposed, but he couldn't help thinking that after what had happened last night, she felt uneasy around him.

Neither of them had mentioned their brief but heated encounter in the moonlight, yet he suspected that it was bothering her.

And he could see why it might. Betsy had come alive in his arms. He'd felt her passion, heard her ragged breathing when she'd come up for air.

She'd been just as aroused as he'd been. And that single kiss had convinced him that their lovemaking would be out of this world.

Of course, she'd said it shouldn't have happened. But it had.

He stole a glance across the seat, as she held on to the steering wheel and peered out the windshield. She'd put on makeup today and had dressed casually. But her expression was as tense and guarded as her grip on the wheel.

More than anything he wanted to put her at ease, to tell her that it had only been a kiss and that they should just take each day as it came.

He wasn't sure how to broach the subject, though, or how to address the obvious chemistry that simmered between them. So he focused on the here and now. "I really appreciate the ride, Betsy."

"No problem." She kept her eyes on the road, her hands on the wheel.

She seemed to have full control of the vehicle. Was she doing the same with her thoughts?

"I have plans with my parents," she added. "So I won't be able to take you back to the ranch right away. I hope you don't mind waiting for me."

"Not at all. I'm in no hurry. I'll just hang out in town until you're finished."

She shot a glance his way and a slow smile eased the tension from her pretty face. "You know, you might not have to wait for us. I've heard that Jim Kelso is always running late. There's no telling how long you'll be in his office."

It irritated him when people couldn't keep to a schedule or when they weren't prompt...

His thoughts froze before he could continue and jumbled before he could grasp the how and why.

As a result of the memory misfire, he clamped his mouth shut, giving in to discouragement and silence.

Ten minutes later, Betsy pointed out Shady Glen, the retirement complex where her parents lived. The fairly new redbrick building was several stories high, with flower gardens and a water fountain in the center of a circular drive.

But she passed by it and pulled into the driveway of a gray medical building adjacent to the hospital.

"See?" she said. "It's just a little over a block away from Dr. Kelso's office."

He opened the passenger door and slid out of the car. "Thanks for the ride. I'll head over to the retirement home when I'm finished and wait for you in the lobby."

"Good idea. They have plenty of sofas and chairs, a cozy fireplace and a big-screen TV. It'll be a perfect place for us to meet later."

"That'll work." He tossed her a don't-worry-about-me grin. "Take your time. And have fun."

As he turned toward the entrance to the medical building, she drove off. But he couldn't help looking over his shoulder to steal one last peek at her, missing what little connection they had. Then he entered the building and sought the directory.

Neurology Associates was in number 206, so he took the elevator to the second floor and found the office. When he reached the front desk, the receptionist, a dishwater blonde in her mid-forties looked up and cast him a sympathetic frown. "I'm really sorry, but Dr. Kelso was just called to the hospital on an emergency. I've been contacting his patients with appointments this morning, but I'm afraid I wasn't able to catch you in time."

He'd hoped Dr. Kelso would tell him that he could return to all of his normal activities—whatever they were. But apparently, that wasn't going to happen today.

Masking his disappointment, he rescheduled the appointment. Then, with nothing else to do, he headed for the retirement home down the street.

The wintry air was crisp, and he shoved his hands into the pockets of the corduroy jacket Doc had loaned him. On the left side, he found a quarter that his bene-factor had left behind.

As he fingered the coin, a niggle of uneasiness settled over him. He wasn't comfortable taking handouts. He wasn't sure how he knew that. But he did.

And while he was glad to have a job and a place to live, he couldn't help feeling as though he needed to pay his own way.

When he turned into the complex, he headed toward a pair of glass doors that opened up to the lobby. The spacious room, with its hardwood floor, cream-colored walls and decor in shades of green and brown, wasn't much different than that of a hotel.

The overstuffed furniture in coordinating fabric provided a homey appearance. And a large brick fireplace, with colorful needlepoint stockings hanging from the mantel and gas flames licking over fake logs, gave the place a cozy, Christmassy feel.

In the far corner, he spotted a large Scotch pine, fully decorated and loaded with sparkling white lights. He wished he could conjure some of the holiday spirit himself, but he came up blank.

Had he been ready for Christmas when he first came to town? When his past hadn't been a mystery to him?

He supposed it didn't matter.

As he continued into the lobby, he noticed a bulletin board next to an unmanned concierge desk. The board was adorned with a snowflake trim and bore several flyers. Curious, he made his way toward it and read the notices that announced a bingo game on Tuesday night, a day trip to the museum in Houston next week and karaoke sing-alongs in the recreation room every Saturday night.

Betsy had been right. This wasn't a hospital, and her parents probably did enjoy living here.

As he started for an empty easy chair near a big-screen television, he figured he was in for a long wait, which was okay with him.

But he'd only taken two steps when the elevator doors opened and Betsy stepped out with a silver-haired couple.

When recognition dawned on her face, he tossed her a grin and shrugged. "My appointment was canceled."

"That's too bad." As she approached him, her parents, a couple in their seventies, came with her.

"It is a little annoying to think I made the trip for nothing, but those things happen. I rescheduled my appointment for later in the week." He nodded toward the television. "I'll just wait here for you to get back."

"Betsy, is this a friend of yours?" her father asked, eyeing John carefully.

When Betsy said that he was, the older man with thinning hair broke into a grin and reached out his arm in the customary greeting. "It's nice to meet you, son. I'm Pete Nielson. And this is my wife, Barbara."

John shook the older man's hand, but he didn't offer a name for himself. What was he supposed to say, "I'm John Doe"?

Fortunately, Betsy stepped in and saved him by offering a discreet, yet truthful, explanation. "This is John. He's staying on Dr. Graham's ranch."

"It's nice to meet you," Pete said. "And although it's

too bad your appointment was canceled, you're just in time for lunch."

"Oh, no," John said. "I don't want to horn in."

"Don't be silly." Barbara placed a hand on his arm. "Any friend of Betsy's is a friend of ours. We'd love to have you join us. Besides, it'll be nice for Pete to have another man to talk to."

John would have jumped at the chance to join Betsy and her parents for lunch, but he didn't have a wallet, a credit card or a penny to his name. And he wasn't used to free rides…

Again, he was caught up in a fact that had no basis for that conclusion, no reason to give that passing thought any credibility.

"You don't need to include me," he said. "I can keep myself busy for an hour or two."

"That's up to you," Betsy said. "But you're welcome to join us. And my mom's right. Daddy is always out-numbered whenever the three of us get together."

"Well," he said, "the problem is that I don't have my wallet with me."

"Don't worry about that," Pete said. "I've got lunch covered today. You can pick up the tab next time."

"Okay. If that's the case, then you've got yourself a deal."

"Glad to hear it," Pete said, a grin spreading across his face as he patted John on the back.

Barbara was smiling, too—as if his company would be a real treat.

John shot a glance at Betsy, to see if she was as happy as her parents seemed to be. But she wore the same unreadable expression she'd had on earlier.

\* \* \*

As Betsy slid into a corner booth at Caroline's Diner with her parents and John, she was both pleased and discomfited about his joining them for lunch. She could have dealt with one or the other, but the conflicting emotions made her uneasy.

Now here they were, seated at the table with their sodas before them and waiting for the waitress to serve their hamburgers.

Her father—a retired banker—leaned toward John and said, "Tell us a little about yourself, young man. What kind of work do you do? And how did you come to meet Dr. Graham?"

Betsy glanced at John, who'd yet to respond, and watched the dilemma weighing in his eyes. But before she could field the question for him, he answered her father truthfully. "Actually, sir, I had an accident a while back and suffered a head injury. I'm afraid I've got temporary amnesia, so there's not much I can tell you."

"I'm so sorry to hear that," Betsy's mother said. "That must be so difficult for you."

"It's tough, but I'm dealing with it."

For a moment, pain shadowed John's eyes. As Betsy's heart went out to him, he rallied and changed the subject. "I was pleasantly surprised when I entered the Shady Glen lobby. It's got a warm and cozy feel about it."

"We like it," her dad said. "And there's a convalescent facility right next door, if one of us should ever need it. But the residents on our side of the complex are considered active seniors, and we have a lot of opportunities to get out on our own and with the others.

I even have a couple of golfing buddies who play with me on Saturdays at a little executive course in Wexler. And Barb belongs to a book club and a quilting group that keeps her busy."

Her mother added, "Betsy wanted us to live with her, but we didn't want to be a burden."

Actually, they'd been afraid they would get in the way if she ever started dating again. But that wasn't going to happen. She'd given up the white-picket-fence dream for herself.

Still, each time she looked at John, she found herself wondering if she'd been wrong. If she could have both a career and a family and balance them as well as Molly Mayfield seemed to have done so far.

But considering something like that, especially with John Doe, was crazy. Look how wrong she'd been about Doug and she'd known him for years.

Sure, they'd been happy at first—or at least she'd thought they'd been. But she'd been so busy with her studies and then with her internship at Grace Memorial that she hadn't realized that while she was working the night shift, her husband hadn't been home in bed.

At least not alone.

And the fact that there had been numerous affairs during their three years together had been worsened by his criminal activity. The conviction for insider trading had left her feeling stupid and naive, confirming to her that the man she'd once thought she loved hadn't been the man she'd thought he was.

Of course, John wasn't anything like Doug.

*Oh, yeah?* a small voice asked. *How in the world could you possibly know* that?

She had nothing to go on but feelings and gut instinct. And when it came to romance and judging a man's character, her emotional gauge had proven to be flawed in the past. Could she ever trust it again?

"Here we go," the waitress said, as she brought a tray with their plates.

"Would you look at those burgers and fries," her father said. "What'd I tell you? Caroline sure knows how to make them right."

As much as Betsy wanted to focus on her meal and to take part in the chatter around her, she couldn't seem to keep her eyes off John. Her curiosity and interest in him were growing by leaps and bounds, especially after that kiss, and she had no idea what to do about it.

So as a result, she remained fairly quiet over lunch, while her father and John seemed to hit it off.

John seemed to know quite a bit about sports and economics, and she wondered if being around her dad might trigger his memory.

Or had it done so already?

When everyone had finished eating and the waitress had picked up the plates, her father asked for the check.

"Don't forget," John said, "I owe you a meal, Pete."

Her dad slid out from his inside seat at the booth, and before heading for the cashier, he tapped his index finger on his temple. "I won't forget. And I'll look forward to next time."

Betsy told herself that John's insistence to pay his own way was a good thing, a sign that he was a decent person at heart. And she reminded herself that some of her assumptions about him were based upon observations she'd made and not just on emotion.

After her father paid the bill, they climbed into her car and headed back to the retirement home. Before she knew it, she was dropping her folks off in front of the lobby doors.

John climbed out to help her mom with the walker—another sign of his character.

"It was nice meeting you," her mother told John. "I hope we get a chance to see you again one day soon."

He smiled. "I'd like that, Barbara."

When they'd all said their goodbyes, she drove away, feeling a bit relieved. John and her parents had hit if off better than she'd expected.

She had to admit, she felt a lot more comfortable with John on the drive back to the ranch than she had coming to town. She wasn't sure why that was, though. Nothing had really changed.

"Your parents are great," he said.

"I think so, too."

"They're really proud of you."

"Yes, they are." In fact, just the other day, her mom had told her that they'd been blessed the day they'd adopted her. And Betsy felt the same way.

She had no idea what her life would have been like if she hadn't grown up in the Nielsons' home.

Yet whenever that question came to mind, she couldn't help wondering about her birth mother, the woman who wanted to meet her. The woman who'd at least taken time to look at her red-haired newborn before handing her over to social workers.

She tried to imagine the possible scenarios that might

have caused the woman to put her newborn daughter up for adoption. A teenage pregnancy? Illegitimacy?

How would the woman feel when she learned that the baby she'd given away had grown up to be happy, successful and well-adjusted?

Would she have been pleased by the decision she'd made? Relieved?

Would she feel disappointed that she hadn't played even the slightest role in Betsy's life?

"It's nice that your parents opted to live in a retirement community rather than become a burden," John said, interrupting her tumble of thoughts.

"They'd never be a burden to me, and I think they know that. In reality, I think they were afraid that if they moved in with me, they'd scare off any potential suitors." She chuckled at their reasoning and turned to John. "They're still concerned that I'll become an old maid."

As their gazes locked, something surged between them, causing her heart to race.

John's voice dropped a decibel, as he said in a husky tone, "There's no chance of that, Betsy."

Her heart zinged as she considered the subtext, but she forced herself to turn away and watch the road before they ended up in a ditch or wrapped around a telephone pole.

Yet in spite of her better judgment, she found herself fishing for the words he'd implied but hadn't actually said. "Why do you say that?"

"Because some lucky guy is going to talk you into marrying him one of these days."

The thought of marriage to a man who truly appreciated her set her heart off-kilter. She tried to remind herself that she was happy being single. At least, she had been until John entered her life.

But ever since they'd kissed last night, she'd found herself envisioning a two-story house in town, surrounded by the proverbial white picket fence. She could imagine a swing hanging from the branch of a tree in the front yard and a set of rocking chairs on the front porch.

She'd always wanted a family—a husband and kids. But her life was cut out for something bigger. Something better.

Or had she just convinced herself of that?

## Chapter Seven

On the way back to Doc's ranch, John watched the road ahead, noting the shops and establishments that stretched along Brighton Valley's main drag. Earlier, when he'd told Doc what he thought was wrong with the pickup, the elderly man had given him some cash and asked him to purchase the parts he would need to fix it while he was in town.

Across the street from Sam Houston Elementary School, John spotted a blue-and-yellow sign that advertised auto parts.

"Would you mind stopping at B.J.'s Auto Works for a minute?" he asked Betsy. "I'd like to pick up a starter for Doc's pickup. I think that was the problem I was having with the engine this morning."

"I'd be glad to." She pulled into the driveway and parked in front of the store. "Do you need me to come in and pay for it?"

"Not unless it costs more than the money Doc gave me."

As he was getting out of the car, she said, "I think it's great that you think you can fix Doc's truck. Maybe you're a mechanic."

"I doubt it. I have a feeling that I can handle something simple, but that's about it."

She paused for a beat, then said, "Your hands were neat and clean when you came into the E.R., so maybe it's safe to assume that you don't fix engines on a regular basis."

"Then maybe I have a white-collar job. Who knows?" He tried to laugh it off, but the fact that he didn't have a clue how he'd been supporting himself before landing in Brighton Valley made any humor in the situation fall flat.

He shut the passenger door, then went into the store. Several minutes later, he returned with a large box filled with his purchases.

"I thought you only needed a starter," she said. "What else did you get?"

"I picked up some oil and filters, too. I'm going to do what I can to get that truck running smoothly for Doc, but if this doesn't do the trick, then he'll have to call in an expert."

John placed the box in the backseat of her car, and once he was buckled in, Betsy took off.

When they arrived at the ranch, she parked near the guesthouse. "Good luck getting Doc's truck started."

"Thanks. What are you going to do this afternoon?"

"I've got some bills to pay, my checkbook to balance and some bookwork to do."

He hoped he would see her later. It wasn't often that she got a day off. And even though his plans would be taken up with repairing Doc's truck, he wondered if she'd remembered his invitation to go riding, a question he'd asked before that mind-blowing kiss.

Maybe it would pan out someday. But for now, they each went their own way.

The first thing John did was to find Doc and tell him he was home. Then he set about replacing the old starter with the new one. While he was at it, he changed the oil and the filters, too. And when he was finished, he opened the back door, entered the service porch and washed the grease and grit from his hands.

Doc, who'd just entered the kitchen, asked, "Have you got the truck running again?"

"Yes, and it started right up."

As John reached for a paper towel to dry his hands, he studied the older man, who seemed out of character dressed in a clean white shirt and a neatly pressed pair of slacks.

"What're you up to?" he asked the man who'd recently showered and shaved.

Doc opened the pantry and pulled out a bottle of red wine that had been lying on its side. "I was invited to have dinner with Edna Clayton, an old friend of mine. And I didn't want to go empty-handed."

"You've been holding out on me, Doc." John crossed his arms, cocked his head to the side and grinned. "You've got a lady friend."

The old man rolled his eyes. "No, I don't."

"I think it's great if you *do*," John said.

"Well, to be honest, Edna and I tiptoed around a romance at one time. I suppose it would have been nice to find love in the golden years, but we never had that kind of spark between us."

"That's too bad."

"Isn't it?" Doc chuckled. "But Edna's a real hoot and a good friend. She's also one heck of a cook. And she's having pork roast and mashed potatoes tonight."

"Have fun."

"I will. But before she called, I put a couple of chicken breasts in the oven to bake. Can you take them out for me? They'll be ready in about thirty minutes or so."

"Sure."

"You know," Doc said, brightening, "why don't you invite Betsy to come over and eat with you?"

A grin tugged at John's lips. "That would be nice. And neighborly."

Doc opened the pantry door and pulled out another bottle of wine, that one a white—pinot grigio.

"Why don't you serve this?" Doc put it in the refrigerator to chill. "It'll go well with the chicken."

It would go well with candles and a little mood music, too. The possibilities were opening up by the minute.

"Thanks," John said. "I think I'll head over there and ask her to dinner now."

He hoped she would agree because he'd like to spend the evening with her.

And have her all to himself.

Betsy had hung up the telephone and was pondering the conversation she'd just had with Roy Adkins, a private investigator, when a knock sounded.

She still held the portable receiver in her hand when she crossed the small living room to see who'd stopped by to see her. She never had company drop by without an invitation, so she figured it had to be either John or Doc.

And she was right. As she swung open the door, John stood on her porch wearing a heart-stopping grin.

"Have you started dinner yet?" he asked.

"No. Why?"

"Because Doc put some chicken in the oven, then got a better dinner offer and took off. Do you want to join me?"

"Sure, why not? I have some vegetables I can make. I'll bring them over to Doc's and fix them there. Just give me a minute."

As John scanned the inside of her living room, with its new pale green love seat and the matching chair upholstered in a floral print, she realized he hadn't been inside the guesthouse before.

"You can come in, if you like, but I'll just be a minute." She lifted the telephone receiver she still held. "Oops, I'd better put this away first."

"Did you want to make a call? I can take the vegetables with me, and you can come over when you're finished."

"Actually, the call just ended. It was the private investigator Carla hired to find me."

"Carla?"

"My biological mother. I guess she wasn't happy with the answer I gave her attorney a couple of weeks ago—that I didn't want to set up a meeting just yet. She's eager to talk to me, but I told the investigator the same thing I told her attorney. I'm stretched to the limit right now and don't want to set a date or time." Betsy put the receiver back in the cradle. "Wait here. It'll just take me a minute to get the veggies."

She went into the kitchen, picked out a ripe tomato, an onion, several zucchinis, a small package of frozen corn and some low-fat cheddar cheese.

When she returned, John was still standing on the porch. "I'm surprised you put off meeting her. If I was approached by a family member, I'd jump on it."

Under the circumstances, she was sure that he would. But her situation was different.

As they headed outside, the sun was setting, taking away the last bit of warmth in the day.

"I'd like to meet her," Betsy admitted, "but my life is complicated these days…." And, truthfully, she wasn't sure when it would be any better.

A bevy of goose bumps lit on her arms, which she suspected was a result of the half-truth she'd told the investigator and had just repeated to John.

He didn't question her comment, and she was glad that he hadn't. The fact was, she was downright afraid to meet Carla and open up her life—and that of her parents—to a complete stranger.

How would she feel upon meeting the woman who'd given her up? How would any of them feel?

She stole another glance at John, realizing that one stranger at a time was about all she could handle, all she would risk.

But the call from Mr. Adkins had given her another idea, and she'd pondered hiring her own investigator to search for John's roots. But at this point, she wouldn't go that far. Still, she was eager for his memory to return. Maybe when he found his identity and remembered his past, it would settle her uneasiness about getting physically—and *emotionally*—involved with a man she really didn't know.

As they crossed the front lawn, John pointed toward the pasture. "Do you see that palomino mare and the roan gelding grazing over there?"

"Yes, that's Buck and Sadie. What about them?"

His steps slowed, and as he studied the horses in the pasture, a look crossed his face that she almost considered a yearning. And an appreciation for horses maybe.

"I talked to Doc about this already," John said, "and one of these days I'm going to take the gelding for a ride. Sadie would be perfect for you, if you still want to go along."

"That sounds like fun. But where did you learn to ride?"

He shrugged. "I...don't know."

"Maybe you're from Texas," she said.

"Maybe."

Of course that was still anyone's guess.

"I was working with them yesterday," John said, "and I had a... Well, I can't exactly call it a memory, but it was a piece of one. I remember riding along an equestrian trail, enjoying a sunset and feeling the ocean breeze on my face."

"You might have experience on a ranch."

"It seems like it."

"And ocean breezes would limit the states that you're from."

He turned to her, that sense of yearning gone. "But not nearly enough. There are a lot of states that border an ocean. And I could have been on vacation."

So they still had nothing concrete to go on.

They continued on their way. Once inside Doc's kitchen, Betsy checked the chicken roasting in the oven, as well as the potatoes Doc had added, deciding dinner was nearly done.

Next, she washed the vegetables, chopped them into chunks and sautéed them in olive oil with a little salt and pepper. As the veggies were starting to soften, she added grated cheese on top and covered the skillet with a lid.

"I'll set the table," John said. "And since Doc suggested we try the pinot grigio with dinner and put it in the refrigerator to chill, I'll uncork the bottle."

"That sounds nice. I can't remember the last time I had a glass of wine with dinner." Or when she'd had a quiet meal with a man whose smile seemed to turn her inside out.

Before long, dinner was ready, and they were both seated at Doc's dining-room table, where John had lit a couple of tapered candles. It was a romantic touch, and she wondered why John had lit them.

Was he a romantic at heart?

Or was he just trying to provide her with a special evening?

She ought to ignore the romantic aura, but she couldn't help appreciating it—and even basking in it.

"The chicken is really tasty," John said. "And while I'm not usually a big fan of vegetables, these are really good." He looked up, his gaze catching hers. Instead of the usual heart-strumming intensity in his eyes, she could see frustration on his brow.

"I keep remembering all kinds of insignificant things," he said, "but nothing that's actually helpful."

"Your memory will come back to you."

"Yeah. But when?"

Betsy rested her forearms on the table and her shoulders slumped ever so slightly. "I wish I had the answer."

With the truth of her statement ringing in their ears, they continued to eat and enjoy their wine in relative silence. When they finished, Betsy helped John with the dishes.

"I have next Sunday off," she finally said. "So unless something changes and I get called in to cover someone's shift, I'm going to have my parents over for an early dinner. Do you want to join us? I'll be inviting Doc, too."

"Thanks, I'd like that. But make a grocery list and let me pick up the food for you. I owe your dad a meal, and I'll have my first paycheck by then, according to Doc. He's insisting on paying me for fixing the truck and being his ranch hand."

"I'm not going to let you spend your first check on groceries. Maybe next time, okay?"

He hesitated a moment, then finally said, "All right."

Betsy really hadn't planned to include John in activities with her family again, especially when there was so much she still didn't know about him. But because pieces of his past had already come back to him while being on the ranch, like a familiarity with horses, she found herself thinking that being around her mom and dad might stir his memory about his own parents.

At least that's the excuse she gave herself. But as they stood at the sink together, he lifted a handful of bubbles and blew them at her, showing her a playful side of him. She couldn't help flicking her fingers, splattering water droplets and foam his way.

They both laughed, and she realized that her efforts to keep him at arm's distance were failing miserably.

She was becoming emotionally involved with John, whether she wanted to or not, and she struggled with what she ought to do about it.

When they had the kitchen put back in order, she was tempted to make an excuse to stick around awhile longer. But instead, she told him she was going to go home, that she wanted to turn in early for the night.

"Okay, then I'll walk you home."

"You don't need to do that."

"I know." His gaze enveloped her, wrapping her up in some kind of electrically charged force field, protecting her it seemed. And suddenly, a whole lot of things didn't seem to matter anymore.

How could she *not* be right about him? How could he *not* have a romantic and protective nature?

So she dropped any and all objections as she headed for the door with John on her heels.

"Where's your jacket?" he asked.

"I forgot to bring one."

"Then take this." He reached for the coat tree, removed the corduroy jacket he'd been wearing earlier and held it for her while she slipped her arms in the sleeves.

Then he opened the door and waited until she walked outside.

It was dark tonight. A few scattered clouds hid most of the stars and the moon, but they were still overhead, twinkling and casting their celestial glow.

It had been a wonderful evening, and Betsy wasn't ready for it to end.

When her shoulder bumped against him, it took everything she had not to reach for his hand, not to slip her arm through his.

A twig crunched under her foot, and somewhere in the pasture, a horse whinnied.

When they reached the steps to her house, she paused, wanting to prolong their time together. "Thanks for a nice evening."

"The pleasure was mine."

Still, neither of them moved.

His gaze zeroed in on hers, and her heart buzzed with anticipation. She was sorely tempted to make a romantic move but didn't.

Thank goodness she didn't have to.

John placed his hands on her waist and drew her toward him, touching his lips to hers, offering a kiss she knew she really ought to refuse. But she'd be darned if she would deny herself the opportunity to hold him one more time. To feel his mouth pressed on hers, to taste him. To...

Oh, how that man could kiss! Her heart soared, her pulse raced and her knees nearly gave out on her.

When it finally ended, leaving her breathless, he ran his knuckles along the side of her cheek, blazing a trail of heat to her core. It had been so long... Too long.

As her mind swirled with what-ifs, his words whispered over her, low and husky. "Good night, Betsy. Sleep well."

She merely nodded, letting him go, even though every cell in her body was demanding that she invite him in for a nightcap—or whatever else might cross his mind.

John had missed out on one hell of an opportunity last night when he let Betsy go with just a kiss. He knew he could have pressed for more, and by the look in her eyes, she probably would have welcomed it. But in his heart, he sensed that she was treading carefully with him.

And he should take things slow, too. He really didn't know if he was free to pursue her.

Was he married? Engaged? Dating someone special?

Either way, he seemed powerless to stop the growing attraction or the subtle infiltration of her scent and her smile into his thoughts, even when she wasn't around.

Of course, that didn't mean he hadn't been productive. Doc's truck was running like a charm now, thanks to the new starter. So he'd been able to drive himself to the rescheduled appointment with Dr. Kelso today. Then he'd oiled the hinges on the barn door and repaired the broken latch on the corral. Doc had quite a few fix-it projects, and John had gotten a good number of them done this week.

Now, here he was, as usual, waiting for Betsy to come home.

She'd been working the day shift this past week,

but she was still away from the ranch from dawn until dusk.

So after he'd shooed Doc out of the kitchen and washed the dishes, he'd gone out to the front porch and took a seat in one of the rockers to wait for Betsy to come home.

And just as he'd learned to expect, she arrived a little after seven-thirty, parked her car and joined him. She was wearing a white lab coat over a black pantsuit, and her curls had been swept up into an attractive twist—the kind a man might like to unpin and let fall down around her shoulders.

Maybe it was her hairstyle or the clothing she was wearing instead of her usual scrubs, but she seemed to be more dressed up than usual.

"So how did your appointment go today?" she asked, as she took a seat in the empty rocker and set it in motion.

"Physically, I'm doing fine. But I still can't remember anything other than a few fleeting images here and there."

Dr. Kelso hadn't seemed too bothered by that, and following an exam, told John he was doing great otherwise.

"No more limitations?" she asked.

"Well, he doesn't want me involved in any strenuous activity or contact sports for another week or so. But I can pretty much do anything else."

For some reason, when the doctor had mentioned activity, the only physical endeavor that came to mind was sex. And the only woman he could imagine taking to bed was Betsy. So he'd specifically asked Dr. Kelso about making love, just in case Betsy had been holding back out of concern for his well-being.

The doctor had given his okay, but that would be John's ace in the hole. There wasn't any reason for Betsy to think that he was hoping their next heated kiss would evolve into more.

So they enjoyed the night sounds for a while and made small talk. Still, he couldn't help deciding that Betsy had been unusually quiet tonight.

"Is something bothering you?" he asked.

Silence enveloped them for a moment. Then Betsy slowed her rocking motion. "There was a hospital board meeting this afternoon, and things got a little tense. I'm afraid the medical center is struggling financially and may not be able to stay afloat another year."

"What happened? Mismanagement of funds?"

She shook her head. "It's complicated. But the biggest problem is that the community wasn't quite large enough to support a medical facility when it was first built."

"Sounds like a mistake in planning," he said, thinking someone who got paid very well to avoid that sort of thing had dropped the ball.

"Maybe so, but the population and demographic projections show that it's just a matter of time when it will be. So the only thing we can do is to wait it out and hope we can stay afloat and hold our own until then."

John stole a glance at Betsy, saw her brow furrowed, her mind clearly burdened. He didn't like seeing her worried about something she couldn't do anything about. As an outsider looking in, it seemed to him that the investors had a lot more to worry about than she did.

"If the hospital has to close its doors," he said, "you'll find other work. You're a skilled doctor and you've established a name for yourself in town. You shouldn't have any problem if you go back to private practice."

"Thanks for the vote of confidence."

She glanced down at the hands in her lap—gifted hands, talented hands. And when she looked up, worry was still splashed across her face.

The hospital, he realized, was her life. But that was sad. A woman like Betsy deserved to have it all—love, marriage, kids if she wanted them.

Not that she should give up a career to do that. A lot of women managed to juggle both just fine, and he suspected that she could be one of them.

Unless, of course, she didn't want to be. And she was the only one who held the answer to that. So he decided to bide his time and see what she would reveal.

Betsy wasn't sure why she'd confided as much as she had in John. It's not as though he could help her with the solution to her problems. But for some reason, she found herself sharing things with him anyway.

Of course, she didn't want to tell him that she'd invested her life savings in the hospital. Not when most people in Brighton Valley thought she was just a dedicated doctor who worked morning and night for the benefit of her patients and the community at large.

"Would it help if the hospital got a loan?" he asked.

"Maybe." She would loan them the money herself, if

she could, but she was stretched to the limit right now. She'd invested everything in the hospital, and thanks to Doug, that "everything" was nearly five hundred thousand dollars.

Doug had been brilliant when it came to buying the right stocks and knowing when to sell, so she'd received a respectable settlement when they divorced.

Normally conservative herself, she'd planned to open a money-market account. But then she'd remembered Doug talking about a good investment in a new pharmaceutical company. She'd heard of the firm and she'd had some knowledge of their research team and the work they were doing. So she'd taken the bulk of her settlement and purchased stock while the price was low.

Betsy wasn't a gambler by nature, but she really didn't consider that particular investment to be all that risky. And her purchase paid off.

When several investors decided to build the Brighton Valley Medical Center, Betsy joined them as a silent partner—putting the bulk of the money gained from selling her stock into the venture. Then she poured her blood, sweat and tears into the hospital.

"To make matters worse," she finally admitted, deciding to share it all, "I'm actually one of the investors in the hospital. So I have more than just a professional interest in its success. I've got a personal interest, too."

"No wonder you're worried."

"Yes, but it's even more than that. I've come to love the people in the area, and I'm concerned about the type of medical care they'll receive if the hospital has to shut down. They used to have to drive all the way to Wexler for X-rays, lab work and surgery. And just shaving the time off an ambulance ride has saved several lives already."

"Maybe the hospital board of directors needs to hire a financial consultant to come in and help them run things a little more efficiently."

She appreciated John's concerns, but other than listening to her vent about things she'd be better off holding close to the vest, there wasn't anything he could do to help.

Deciding to avoid letting the conversation get any deeper, she feigned a yawn.

"Tired?" he asked.

"I'm exhausted. I didn't get much sleep last night."

"Do you want me to walk you home?"

She really ought to tell him no, but her answer rolled out before she had a chance to think it through. "Sure, if you'd like to."

As she stood, he got to his feet, too. Then they started across the lawn to the guesthouse, where the automatic timer had already turned on the porch light to illuminate their path.

Would he try to kiss her again?

And if so, would she let him?

She knew that she had no business allowing things to get physical between them when the only things she had to go on when assessing his character were hunches and hormones.

How could she trust emotion to help her make a rational decision?

Yet as they reached her front door, her heart was already slipping into overdrive and the pheromones were swirling overhead.

As John pulled her into his arms, he searched her face as if looking for something.

For an objection? she wondered. If so, he wouldn't get one from her now. Not when all she wanted was to feel his mouth on hers.

So she wrapped her arms around his neck and drew his lips to hers.

As their bodies pressed together, taking up where they'd left off last night, their hands began to stroke, to explore. As he reached her breast, as his thumb skimmed across her nipple, an ache settled in her most feminine parts.

This was so not a good idea. But how in blazes could she put a stop to it when her body was screaming for more?

Yet when they finally broke away to catch their breaths, when they both had to hold on to each other as if they'd collapse in a heap if they didn't, Betsy finally took a step back, providing the distance needed to separate.

"I'm glad your memory loss didn't include kissing," she said, trying to make light of the passion that blazed between them.

His eyes, hooded with desire, locked on hers. "I didn't forget what comes next, either."

She was sure that he hadn't.

The invitation to come inside the house and show her all that he remembered hovered over them, yet she couldn't quite bring herself to ask him in.

Despite her fears, she was falling for John Doe.

What in the world was she going to do if he proved to be less than the man she hoped him to be?

## Chapter Eight

Ten days and two paychecks later, John had settled into the ranch and had tackled all the chores that had been expected of him and several fix-it projects he'd found on his own.

At first, he'd thought that Doc had offered him a place to stay and a job out of the goodness of his heart. And while that was probably a big part of it, John had soon come to realize that there was more going on than that.

Over the past couple of years, Doc had sold off several parcels of land, as well as a lot of his stock. But he was still having a hard time keeping up with the daily work and the regular maintenance of the ranch.

That shouldn't be surprising, though. Dr. Graham was pushing ninety and, as a result, was slowing down.

The elderly physician knew it, too. He and John

had even talked about it briefly over breakfast this morning.

As he'd poured himself a cup of fresh coffee, Doc had said, "I'm thinking about selling this place."

The man's comment had surprised John, although he wasn't sure why. "If you do decide to sell, where will you go?"

Doc carried his mug back to the table and sat across from John. "Have you ever heard of Shady Glen?"

"Yes, I've even been inside the lobby."

Doc took a sip of coffee. "It's not a bad place. In fact, I know quite a few people there, including Pete and Barbara Nielson. And everyone seems to like it."

"Are you thinking about moving into one of the senior apartments?" John asked.

"That's certainly crossed my mind. I may not like facing my physical limitations, but I need to. It happens to all of us eventually. Besides, I don't have much family left, just a couple of nephews who live out of state. And as much as I've come to think of Betsy as my daughter, she really isn't. So why burden her?"

John had come to know Betsy pretty well, so he didn't think he was out of line when he said, "I don't think she'd mind."

"Maybe not. But even her own parents know that she works too hard as it is. And that she wouldn't have a life at all if she had to take care of them."

Doc had a point. Betsy had taken up the slack again this week at the hospital when one of the E.R. residents had broken his leg skiing on Saturday. So neither John nor Doc had seen very much of her.

She'd even had to cancel that Sunday dinner she'd

wanted to have with her parents, thanks to a cocky young intern who should have stuck to the bunny slopes and not tried to hotdog it.

Of course, that didn't mean John hadn't seen her at all. After dinner each night, when Doc had retired to his room and curled up with a good book, John had gone out to the porch and waited until Betsy came home from work. Then they'd hung out for a while and talked about their days.

It had become an evening ritual, he supposed. After a while, Betsy would make an excuse to go home, and he'd walk her to the door. Then he'd kiss her good-night, something they both clearly enjoyed.

Trouble was, each kiss seemed to be more heated and more demanding than the last, which was a damn good sign that the two would be good together in bed. But Betsy had continued to hold back, to keep things from getting out of hand.

John couldn't blame her for that, he supposed. But he was ready to take their relationship to a sexual level, and it was getting to the point that he'd have to suggest something to her pretty soon. Maybe even tonight.

A plan began to form—a quiet dinner, a glass of wine. Candles, some soft romantic tunes.

He had her cell-phone number, so he would call her later and tell her not to eat before coming home. Then, after lunch, he would borrow Doc's truck, drive to the market and pick up everything he needed to make a special dinner for two.

He wasn't sure what he'd fix, though. Maybe tacos. He'd been craving some good Mexican food lately. He hadn't had any since…

Well, it had been ages, he supposed, as he socked away yet another vague and useless recollection.

As he reached for another nail to hammer into the loose porch railing, he pondered taking Betsy out to dinner instead. He'd seen a restaurant in town called La Cocina, which translated to The Kitchen in English.

His movements froze. How had he known that? Was he bilingual? Or had he just taken Spanish in school and been left knowing some of the basics?

Was he Latino?

Whenever he looked into the mirror, he thought he might have Hispanic bloodlines. Had he learned English as a second language? Was he craving the type of food he'd grown up eating?

At this point, he had absolutely no way of knowing, and frustration rose inside of him. He tried to release it with each swing of the hammer, each pound on the nail, but he wasn't having much luck.

He had, however, fixed the railing in no time flat.

As his stomach growled, he looked up at the sun, which was high in the winter sky and starting a slow descent. Was it after noon already? Doc hadn't called him in for lunch yet.

It wasn't any big deal, he supposed. But he set the hammer in the toolbox and went into the house.

"Doc?" he called.

No answer.

When he reached the living room and spotted the old man lying on the floor, his heart dropped to his gut.

"Oh, God." He hurried to the Doc's side. "What's the matter? Are you okay?"

Doc's lips quivered, but he didn't speak.

John hurried to the phone and dialed 9-1-1. When the dispatcher answered, he explained the situation and requested an ambulance and immediate help. Then he called Betsy on her cell.

"Something's happened to Doc," he said. "I think it's a stroke."

"Did you call the paramedics?"

"They're on their way."

"I'll be waiting for you."

A response wadded up in his throat, so he didn't say anything else. When he ended the call, he sat on the floor next to the elderly man who'd become a friend, hoping that help arrived in time.

John followed behind the ambulance in Doc's pickup, trying to keep up with the emergency vehicle without breaking the law. The paramedics had confirmed what he'd suspected: Doc had suffered a stroke.

As red lights flashed up ahead and the siren blared all around him, a disjointed vision formed in his mind—a black Mercedes, its air bags deployed. A light blue mini-van, broken glass, twisted metal. The cries of a child. Another siren sounding.

John blinked a couple of times, trying to hold on to the images and to make sense of them, but nothing materialized.

Had he been in an accident?

Had he witnessed one?

Damn, the amnesia was getting old. And it frustrated the hell out of him.

He followed the ambulance to the entrance of the medical center, where it turned to the left and headed toward the front doors of the emergency room. John continued on and found a place to park. But by the time he got inside, Doc was already back in one of the exam rooms.

Now what? he wondered, as he scanned the waiting room that was neither full nor empty.

Not all of those seated were patients, but they represented the people Betsy dealt with every day: the worried parents holding a sick feverish toddler; a teenage boy with a gash on his knee; a blue-collar worker with what appeared to be a broken arm.

On the night John had been found beaten in the parking lot of the Stagecoach Inn, he'd probably been rushed through this same room on a gurney. But he had to have been unconscious when they brought him in. The place didn't look even remotely familiar.

Before taking a seat, he wondered if he ought to let Betsy know that he was here, but he didn't want to call her away from Doc. Not while she might be working to save the man's life. So he took a seat near the television, although he didn't give a damn what channel it was on. He couldn't concentrate on anything other than the two double doors that required a security code to get through.

Finally, about twenty minutes later, he spotted Betsy standing behind a glass window where the receptionist sat. She was looking out into the waiting room, and when she spotted him, she waved, then beckoned toward the doorway that led to the exam rooms. He crossed the room and when the doors opened, he joined her.

"The paramedics told me you were driving Doc's

pickup and would be waiting here," she said as she led him through a maze of exam rooms.

"How's he doing?" John asked, keeping step with her.

"I think he's going to be okay, but it'll be a while before we know if there's been any permanent damage. But you got him here quickly, and we've started treatment."

"Are you going to be his doctor?"

"No, I've called in Jim Kelso. We'll know more after he's had a chance to examine him and run the appropriate tests." Betsy entered the break room and indicated that John should take a seat. "It's going to take a while. Do you want some coffee?"

"Sure."

She filled two disposable cups, brought them to the table and handed one to John. Then she took the chair next to his. But instead of taking a drink, she circled her fingers around the foam container, soaking up what little heat it gave out.

Doc didn't have any family members who lived close enough to make decisions, but she was up for the task. In fact, she wouldn't want it any other way.

"When Doc's released from the hospital," she said, "I'm going to have to find a caretaker who can stay with him at the house."

John placed his hand on her forearm and gave it a gentle squeeze. When she looked into his compassionate gaze, her heart took a tumble.

"You don't need to go to the trouble," John said. "I can look after him, but I think he might be ready to move into Shady Glen."

"What makes you say that?" she asked.

"Because we actually talked about that at breakfast this morning. He told me that the ranch was becoming too much for him, and he said he planned to put it on the market. He also mentioned how happy your parents seemed to be at Shady Glen and that he thought he would be, too."

Betsy pondered John's words, realizing that Doc had already contemplated his future, and that the stroke would only force him to make a move sooner than he'd planned.

"I know you'd like to find a way for him to stay at home," John said, his hand still resting on her arm, his body heat warming her to the bone. "But I think he'll fight you on that, honey."

His understanding of the emotions running through her heart, as well as the friendship that had developed between her and her mentor, surprised her. And as a result, she didn't know what to say.

"Doc has accepted the limitations his age has brought about," John added.

"And you're saying that I need to accept it, too?"

He nodded. "That's about the size of it. And I'm sorry."

She took a deep breath, acknowledging the truth of his words, of Doc's situation, then slowly blew it out. "There's an intermediate care facility located right next to the Shady Glen apartments."

"So Doc will be close to your parents, and they can visit him often."

That was true. And the nurses and the staff at Shady Glen were exceptionally kind and loving to the residents.

They never let a holiday go by without decorating and planning various outings and activities to honor that particular day or season.

In fact, the day after Thanksgiving, they put up that big Christmas tree in the lobby. But thoughts of the holidays at Shady Glen took a sad turn.

Last year, Betsy had brought her mom and dad to Doc's house for the day. They'd had a special dinner together, complete with homemade pies from Caroline's. But this year, she wouldn't be cooking. Not if Doc wasn't at home.

There'd be no more Christmas mornings at the ranch, sitting around the tree, enjoying a cozy fire in the hearth, laughing with the three people she loved most in the world.

Betsy, more than anyone, knew that time marched on and that change was inevitable, but she wasn't ready for it. And she wasn't just getting nostalgic about Christmas, either.

If Doc was going to sell the ranch, she'd have to move, which shouldn't be that big of a deal for a woman who spent so little time there. But the little guesthouse had become home to her, a quiet little corner of the world where she could let down her hair and just be herself.

She would have the memories of living on the ranch, of course, but since she'd spent so much of her life burning the candle at both ends, she wouldn't have as many of them as she could have—if she'd stopped long enough to smell the roses.

Tears welled in her eyes, and she struggled to blink

them back. But it was too late. They filled her eyes to the brim and began to roll down her cheeks.

"I'm sorry," John said again, as he lifted his hand and brushed his thumb under her eyes, wiping away her tears.

She managed a smile. "I know. I'm sorry, too."

They sat like that for a while, wrapped in an emotional cocoon and connected in a way that went beyond the physical—the stolen glances, the good-night kisses. Somehow, over the past couple of weeks, they'd become friends—and more.

When one of the licensed vocational nurses came into the break room and removed a yogurt she'd left in the fridge, she froze in her tracks.

"I'm sorry," she said, apparently picking up on the vibes Betsy and John must have been putting out. "Am I interrupting something?"

"No, not at all." Betsy pushed her chair back, got to her feet and, addressing John, said, "I'll be right back. I'm going to check with Dr. Kelso and get a prognosis."

At least, that's the excuse she came up with for gathering up her heart before she threw it at the man, hoping he'd catch it.

And hoping that he'd cherish the gift Doug had taken for granted.

After Betsy had talked to Jim Kelso and learned that Doc's situation seemed a little more promising than it had appeared to be when he'd been brought into the E.R., she'd relayed the prognosis to John.

"Thank God," he'd said, relieved to know the retired

doctor would probably recover—with time and physical therapy.

"They'll be taking him to Intensive Care for a day or so," she'd added, "but that's routine. They want to monitor him closely."

At that point, John could have taken off and gone back to the ranch, he supposed. But the elderly man didn't have any family to speak of, and John figured he could use a friend about now. So he'd waited until Doc was settled in the ICU, then stopped by to see him.

Doc had opened his eyes long enough to acknowledge John's visit. His lips quirked in what might have been a smile, then he'd dozed off.

John stood at his bedside for a while, then told the nurse in charge that he would be back in the morning.

Yet he still didn't leave the hospital. Instead, he called Betsy and told her he was going to wait in the lobby until she was free to leave.

"You've got to be hungry," he told her. "And I'm starving. Let's go out to dinner."

"All right."

He hoped she didn't give him a hard time about picking up the tab tonight. The local bank, where Doc had an account, had allowed him to cash his paycheck without any ID. He'd already made a small payment to the hospital, as well as one to Dr. Kelso. He would pay them more next week, but he'd kept enough to spring for dinner tonight. And that felt good.

At a few minutes after seven, Betsy met John in the lobby. She was wearing her street clothes—black slacks and a pink sweater. She'd also let her hair down—soft curls a man longed to touch.

"You look nice," he told her. She also looked as sexy as hell, but he kept that thought to himself.

"Thanks. I keep a change of clothes in the locker room and decided to wear them tonight. I've been spending most of my waking hours in scrubs."

"Where do you want to eat?" he asked, as they headed for the lobby doors.

"There's an Italian restaurant that just opened up a month or so ago. I've never eaten there before, but I've heard that it's good. What do you think?"

He really didn't have a preference. He'd eat just about anything right now, as long as they offered quick service. "Italian's great."

"We can walk," she said. "It's not very far."

She was right. Cara Mia was located just a couple of blocks down the street. Other than a black awning over the door, the eatery didn't look anything out of the ordinary on the outside. But the inside, with its polished hardwood floors and white walls, was warm and inviting.

Each table, which was draped in crisp white linen, was adorned with a single red rose in a glass bud vase and several lit votives. A stone fireplace in the back, with flames licking over real logs, added to the ambience. And so did a Christmas tree that had been decorated with a variety of colorful ornaments and blinking lights.

Everyone in Brighton Valley seemed to be ready for the holiday, and John realized he was going to have to get with the program. He didn't have much money to spend or more than a couple of gifts to buy, but he wanted to give Betsy something special.

The waiter pointed out the wine list. After a brief perusal, Betsy asked for a glass of sauvignon blanc, and John chose one of his favorite Napa Valley merlots.

When John realized that he'd just remembered yet another inconsequential fact, he kept the news to himself. Why put a damper on the evening by reminding Betsy that he still had no real memory of the life he'd once led?

While the waiter served their drinks, they looked over their menus. Betsy decided on the vegetarian lasagna, and John asked for the chicken marsala.

The prices weren't as steep as John was used to—another tidbit of information that he would have to tuck away—yet even so, the bill would take the bulk of his remaining cash. But he didn't care about that. He wanted the evening to be memorable.

He also wanted to carry his own weight, which had always been important to him.

It was odd, though. There were some things he just seemed to know about himself. And he tried to take comfort in the fact that he had a sense of honor, that he liked the finer things in life and that he paid his own way.

As the candlelight flickered on the table, casting a romantic spell over them, John and Betsy enjoyed a tasty meal.

"Cara Mia was a good choice," John said.

"I think so, too." Betsy scanned the intimate room, with its artsy, European-style prints framed in black and hung upon white plastered walls. "Isn't the ambience great?"

John agreed. "Maybe next time we can try La Cocina, which is just down the street."

"I'd like that. I haven't had good Mexican food for a long time. My ex-husband used to like it, so it was almost a given that we'd have it often. But I kind of swore off of it for a while after he moved out."

She'd told John that her ex-husband hadn't been dedicated to the relationship, but she hadn't gone into detail. He supposed it wasn't any of his business, but he was curious about the guy and about the downfall of their marriage.

"So why did you two split up?" he asked.

She paused, as if he'd tapped a sensitive subject. Then she lifted the linen napkin and blotted her lips. "He was seeing someone else."

He'd had an affair? John couldn't imagine a man doing something like that to Betsy, and his heart went out to her. If he had a wife like her...

Damn. *Did* he have a wife?

He glanced at his left hand, which was resting on top of the linen-covered table. He wasn't wearing a wedding band.

Was that enough to go on?

It was hard to say. It was possible that he'd been wearing a ring, and that it had been stolen along with his wallet and any money or credit cards he'd had when he'd first come to town.

But he didn't see a tan line.

Still, he wasn't going to stress about that now. What if he never got his memory back? What if he was stuck in Brighton Valley for the rest of his life?

Would that be so bad?

Right this minute, as he sat across from Betsy, with violin music playing in the background and candlelight flickering, the answer was a definite no. And he wondered how Betsy would feel about that.

As Betsy studied her handsome dinner companion, she couldn't remember when she'd had an evening as nice as this. And she couldn't help thinking about their trip home tonight.

They would walk back to the hospital and drive to the ranch in separate cars. But then what?

Would John kiss her good-night the way he'd been doing each evening this week? Would either of them press for more than a kiss on the front porch?

She could certainly invite him into the guesthouse for a nightcap. But as she stole a glance at her handsome dinner companion, his smile sent her heart scrambling to right itself, and she realized it wasn't an after-dinner drink that she was craving. It was John.

After he'd paid the bill, they took a leisurely stroll back to the hospital and noted the Christmas decorations in the various store windows.

They turned left at the light and into the parking lot where they'd left their cars. Their arms brushed against each other, and he took her hand in his, warming her from the inside out.

They were dating, she supposed. And while she ought to be at least a little concerned about what that might mean in the future, she couldn't seem to conjure any of the apprehension she'd had when she'd first realized her attraction to him.

Moments later, they reached her car, and she opened the door with the remote.

"I'll follow you home," he said.

She appreciated his protective nature. In fact, there were a lot of things about John that she found appealing. He was bright, kind and thoughtful, a gentleman who knew how to treat a lady.

He was also far too handsome for her own good.

All the way to the ranch, she continued to glance in her rearview mirror, to see John's headlights as he followed at a safe distance behind her.

When they arrived, she parked near the guesthouse, and he pulled up beside her.

Should she invite him to come inside? Or should she wait to see what he suggested?

Before she could decide, he walked up to her, took her by the hand and strode toward her front door, where the yellow glow of the porch light welcomed them home.

"Would you like to come in?" she asked.

"Yeah." He gave her hand a gentle squeeze. "That'd be nice."

His smile and a heated glimmer in his eyes caught her off guard, leaving her a little unbalanced.

Did he have any idea what he did to her?

When they reached the front door, she let him into the living room and turned on the lamp.

Now what? she wondered.

He walked over to the entertainment center, which she didn't use as often as she'd thought she would when she purchased it last summer. Then he turned to her and smiled. "Do you mind if I turn on the radio?"

"No. Go ahead." She dropped her purse on the sofa but continued to watch him.

He fiddled with the knobs and dials for a moment, then tuned in a country-and-western station.

A duet sung by Faith Hill and Tim McGraw was on—a sexually charged love song. He turned to her and grinned, showing off a gorgeous pair of dimples that spun her heart around.

Then he reached out his hand to her. "Dance with me, Betsy."

It wasn't a question, but she wouldn't have declined even if it had been. So she stepped into his embrace, swaying to the beat as Faith and Tim crooned softly in the background.

His cologne, a faint, wood scent, mingled with those ever-present pheromones that taunted her whenever he was near.

As he wrapped his fingers around hers and slipped his arm around her waist, holding her, possessing her, she placed her hand on his chest and felt the warmth of his body, the solid beat of his heart.

She closed her eyes, letting herself go, trusting him. Trusting fate.

His voice, low and husky with desire, whispered against her cheek. "I might not be able to tell you much about the man I am, Betsy, but I know the woman you are. And I'm falling for you."

Oh, God, she thought. She was falling for him, too.

The words of the song, the sensual beat, the man in her arms, all stirred something deep within her core—a sweet ache. A desperation.

She drew away just long enough to look in his eyes,

to catch his expression. And when she did, he lowered his mouth to hers.

As their lips met, separating, their tongues touched, and the warmth of his breath—still laced with the sweetness of the tiramisu they'd shared earlier—nearly buckled her knees.

She kissed him, harder, deeper, until she finally had to stop long enough to catch her breath.

Did she dare tell him what she wanted? What she needed?

Fortunately, she didn't have to because he spoke, his breath warm and ragged against her skin. "I want more than a kiss tonight. But if you don't, then tell me to stop now."

She wanted more, too. So much more. And there was no use denying it or making up an excuse as to why they should sleep alone.

So she made the decision to lay her heart on the line, no matter what the cost. And taking him by the hand, she led him into her bedroom.

## Chapter Nine

As Betsy and John entered her bedroom, he realized she was giving him an incredible gift. If their kisses were any hint of the magic between them, making love was bound to be off the charts.

Yet it was more than sex. Betsy was the kind of woman that men dreamed about.

Now, as they stood beside her queen-size bed, with its white, goose-down comforter looking almost cloudlike, he kissed her again. Softer, sweeter. Then harder and deeper.

As his hands slid along the curve of her back and down the slope of her hips, a surge of desire shot right through him. He pulled her hips forward, against his erection, letting her know how badly he wanted her.

She whimpered into his mouth, then arched forward, revealing her own need, her own arousal.

Had he ever wanted a woman this badly?

When he thought he was going to die from the strength of his desire, she ended the kiss, then slowly removed her pink sweater and dropped it to the floor.

He watched as she unbuttoned her slacks and slid the zipper down in a slow and deliberate fashion. Her gaze never left his as she slipped the fabric over her hips and peeled them off.

Moments later, she stood before him in a pale blue bra and matching panties. Her body, petite yet lithe, was everything he'd imagined it to be and more.

And tonight, she was his.

Following her lead, he unbuttoned his shirt, pulled his arms out of the sleeves, then let the garment fall to the floor. Next, he unbuckled his belt and undid the metal buttons on his Wranglers.

When he'd removed all but his boxers, he eased toward her.

She skimmed her nails across his chest, sending a shiver through his veins and a rush of heat through his blood. Then she unsnapped her bra and freed her breasts, full and round, the dusky pink tips peaked and begging to be touched.

As he bent and took a nipple in his mouth, she gasped in pleasure. He lavished first one breast, and then the other. Fully aroused, she swayed and had to clutch his shoulder to stay balanced, her nails digging into his back.

Taking mercy on her—and on himself—he lifted her in his arms and placed her on top of the bed. Her hair splayed upon the white pillow, her body upon the comforter.

He wanted nothing more than to slip out of his

boxers and feel her skin against his, but he paused for a beat, drinking in the angelic sight. "You're beautiful, Betsy."

A slow smile stretched across her lips. "So are you."

He didn't know about that, but he was glad that she was pleased with what she saw, at what he did to her.

Determined to make sure that it was better than good for her, that she wouldn't have any regrets in the morning, he joined her on the bed, where they continued to kiss, to taste, to stroke each other until they were both drowning in need.

"We have all night," she said, as she pulled free of his embrace. "So we can take things slow and easy later. Right now I need to feel you inside of me."

He didn't want to prolong the foreplay any longer, either. And she was right. They had the rest of the night, and he planned to use every minute of it. Then a practical thought crept in. He had no protection with him.

"But I don't have any—"

"Wait," she said, rolling to the side of the bed. She reached into the nightstand drawer and pulled out a small, unopened box of condoms.

He wasn't sure if she kept them handy just in case, or whether she'd planned for this night to happen. Either way, he was glad she'd been prepared.

Taking the packet she offered him, he tore it open and rolled on the condom. Then, as he hovered over her, she reached for his erection and guided him right where she wanted him to be.

He entered her slowly at first, getting the feel of her, the feel of them. And as her body responded to his, she arched up to meet each of his thrusts, the world stood still and nothing mattered but the two of them and what they were doing to and for each other.

As he reached a peak, she cried out, arched her back and let go. Once her climax began, he shuddered, releasing with her in a sexual explosion that had him seeing stars.

No longer separate bodies, they became one, enjoying each ebb and flow until they were physically spent.

John had no idea what the future would bring, but for now, they belonged together—face-to-face, skin to skin…

Heart to heart.

As dawn broke over the valley, sending long slivers of sunlight through the cracks in the shutters, Betsy woke in John's arms.

She'd hardly slept a wink last night, and she had to go to work today. But that didn't stop a sated smile from stretching across her face and a flood of warmth from spilling over her heart.

Of course, why wouldn't she be feeling pleased and content? Sex with John had been amazing—and far better than she'd ever anticipated it to be.

How many times had they made love last night?

Four or five, she supposed. And each joining had been better than the last.

She hadn't planned on having a lover, hadn't wanted to take the risk. But the longer she'd known John, the deeper her attraction, the less that seemed to matter anymore.

Last night, she'd lowered her guard. And now she was

facing the fact that she'd fallen in love with John, which left her vulnerable to heartbreak and disappointment. But giving him up wasn't an option any longer.

She glanced at the clock on the bureau, saw that it was nearing six. Nature was calling—and so was the E.R. As much as she'd like to, she couldn't stay home any longer. She needed to shower, get dressed and head to the hospital.

She also needed to check in on Doc and see how he was doing. She'd left her number as a family contact, though. And because her phone hadn't rung, she could easily assume that all was well. Still, she wanted to talk to Jim Kelso later this morning, just to be sure there weren't any unexpected complications.

As she carefully pulled away from John's embrace, trying not to wake him, he drew her back into his arms and brushed a kiss on her shoulder. His breath was hot, taunting. And she could feel him stirring behind her, his arousal growing.

She suspected that he could easily be encouraged to make love again. And so could she. But while she was tempted to place that call and feign an illness that would require another E.R. doctor to step in for her, she just couldn't do it. Call her dedicated, responsible or even a control freak, but she couldn't—*wouldn't*—do that to the people who needed her.

"I wish I could stay home," she said, "but the hospital and the patients are counting on me."

"I know." John released his hold, letting her go.

As she slid out of bed, his fingers trailed along her back and down a bare hip, marking her as his. She actually liked the idea of belonging, of being a couple again, especially with him. And again, she felt the invisible bond that drew her to him, a connection that was much stronger after last night.

"I'll put on a pot of coffee," he said. "And I'll fix breakfast while you're in the shower."

She stopped in the middle of the room and turned to face him. "You don't have to do that. I can grab a yogurt and a banana as I go. And there's always coffee in the break room."

"That liquid mud?" He chuckled. "I've tasted it, remember? Go ahead and get ready for work. I'll make myself useful."

Betsy paused long enough to cross her arms and toss a smile his way. "*Actually,* you made yourself pretty darn useful last night."

He sat up in bed, the sheet dropping below his waist. A glimmer lit his eyes and he grinned. "It *was* good, wasn't it?"

Their gazes locked, which made her pause for just a beat. "It was the *best.*"

There hadn't been any reason to keep her opinion to herself. John had figured it out. He'd seen it in her eyes, heard it in her whimpers, felt it in her arms.

As she reached the doorway that led to the hall, a hint of apprehension whispered over her as she thought about what they'd done, about the unspoken commitment they'd made last night.

If truth be told, she'd feel a lot better if she knew who John really was, if she had more details about his past. But she'd seen how good he was with Doc, how good he was with the horses.

How good he'd been with her.

Surely that counted for something.

As she began to pass through the bedroom doorway, she glanced over her shoulder, stealing one last peek at the naked man sitting on the edge of her bed, the tall, dark and handsome stranger who held her heart in his hands.

His smile told her not to worry, that everything would be okay.

She just hoped she could believe that.


As Betsy disappeared down the hall, John waited for the bathroom door to click open and shut. Then he threw off the covers and climbed out of bed.

He wished she'd been able to stay home this morning, but he, more than anyone, understood job obligations and professional commitments. Again, he wasn't sure how he knew that—he just did.

He'd no more than placed a bare foot on the cold hardwood floor when voices from the past blasted through the wall that had been holding back his memories.

*Please don't go,* a woman said. *Not today.*

*I have to. There's an executive board meeting this morning.*

*I don't care about that. Call your secretary and tell her you'll be late. I need an hour of your time, and for once, you need to give it to me.*

The board meeting had been important, though. And his presence was critical. Several attorneys had cleared their calendars for the day just to be on hand.

*I'll tell you what,* he'd said to the woman. *I'll leave the office early. And then we can—*

*No,* she'd shouted, her voice loud, her anger clear.

*Those sweet-talking promises of yours aren't going to work on me anymore, Jason.*

Even now, in Brighton Valley, Texas, John was reeling, trying to make sense of the conversation.

Then her voice dropped to an ominous and threatening decibel, as her threat echoed in his mind. *If you go now, it's over. I'll be gone before you get home.*

He'd never appreciated ultimatums, never fell for them. Not even those issued by...?

Suddenly it was gone—the vague memory, the voices.

Had *he* been the man in question? The one she'd called Jason?

Yes, he had to be. But who was *she?* A girlfriend? A wife?

Had she made good on her promise to move out? Or had John—or rather, Jason—given in to her demands?

And when had that blasted conversation taken place? Last week? Last month? Last year?

He ran a hand through his tousled hair, as if that would clear his mind and gather his thoughts. But it didn't free him from the darkness that had swallowed his memory and had shot his reality full of holes.

More frustrated than ever, he headed for the kitchen, intending to put on a pot of coffee and to fix Betsy something to eat.

At least he could follow up on that particular commitment.

But were there others he should have kept?

Two days later, while sitting in Doc's pickup in the parking lot of Miller's Market, John—or rather,

Jason—didn't have any more answers than he did when he'd remembered that snippet of conversation between him and a yet-to-be-remembered woman.

For that reason, he'd kept the knowledge of that particular memory flash to himself, as well as all the questions it had served to stir up. After all, how could he explain anything to Betsy when he couldn't understand any of it himself?

Still, he'd been relieved to have finally gotten a solid clue to the man he really was. At least he'd thought he had. He'd assumed that he was a businessman of some kind, but then he'd realized that might not be a safe assumption.

What if he'd just needed to attend that board meeting as an invited guest, like the attorneys who'd cleared their calendars?

Apparently, even his most telling revelation to date hadn't been all that helpful.

The morning after he and Betsy had first made love, he'd managed to make coffee, scramble some eggs and send her off to the hospital without her realizing that he was being unusually pensive.

At least she hadn't said anything about it then.

After she'd left for the hospital, he'd kept himself busy. He'd fed the stock, mucked the stalls and rode the perimeter of the ranch, checking the fence for places that needed repair. But in spite of his productivity that day, his mood had been crappy.

But why wouldn't it be? He hadn't been able to figure out what to do about his relationship with Betsy. He'd certainly wanted to make love to her again, but how could he if he wasn't sure if he was involved with someone else or not?

Of course he'd been able to come up with quite a few reasons to believe the woman who'd issued him the ultimatum had done so ages ago. And that he was free to continue a relationship with Betsy.

Trouble was, if he didn't give a rat's ass about the possibility of a prior romantic commitment with someone else, it wouldn't make him any better than Betsy's lousy ex-husband had been.

Still, when she came home that night, he'd been waiting for her on the porch. And after a quiet dinner, they'd gone to bed—together.

The same scene had played out the next night, although he'd found himself growing more and more pensive—and more frustrated by the amnesia that plagued him. In fact, that's why he continued to sit in Doc's pickup, just thinking about the things that were happening in the present.

Betsy hadn't gone in to work today, which was what brought him to the market now.

Earlier, she'd gone to see Doc and had returned to the house with a couple of bags filled with groceries.

"Need some help?" he'd asked, heading toward her.

"No, I've got it."

She'd kissed him, then carried the groceries into the house. "I invited my folks to dinner tonight. I hope you're okay with that."

"Of course." He liked her parents. But he had to admit that he was a little uneasy about making any kind of public statement about their relationship—at least, until he knew where it was going.

Or what might keep it from going anywhere.

"I thought we'd have tacos," she'd said. "How does that sound to you?"

"Great."

As she began to put away her purchases, she paused and looked him over. Really looked. "You've been awfully quiet the past few days. Is something wrong?"

"No," he lied, not wanting to admit that he was burdened by guilt, which could really be for naught.

It was entirely possible that he was unattached. And if he learned that he had a wife or fiancée, he'd end their sexual relationship immediately.

"Are you sure?" she asked.

"I've just got Doc on my mind. I probably should have gone to see him today, but I got caught up with chores and the time just slipped away."

Okay, so that wasn't entirely true. He was concerned about Doc, of course. And he'd been busy. But that wasn't the cause of his silence.

"Doc is actually doing better today," she said.

"I'm glad to hear that." He tossed her a smile, which seemed to put her mind at ease.

Why should they both be miserable and stressed?

"He's having some speech problems," she added, "but he was able to communicate. And you were right. He definitely wants to sell the ranch."

John nodded, his mind still on other concerns, like whether he should come right out and admit what he was struggling with.

"Doc asked if you would oversee things until it's all said and done," she said.

"I'd be happy to. I owe him a lot for providing me with a job and a place to stay."

She seemed pleased with his answer. But he hadn't been blowing smoke. He did feel an obligation to Doc, and he really enjoyed working outdoors.

Was that a contradiction to the theory he'd had about being a businessman?

There was also a part of him that didn't care whether he remembered his past life or not—the part of him that had fallen for Betsy, the part that didn't want to be with another woman, no matter who she was.

"I also stopped by the admission office at the Shady Glen Convalescent Hospital. When Doc is discharged from the medical center, he can transfer there. And once he recovers more fully, he can move into one of the apartments."

"How soon do you think that'll be?"

"If he's lucky, in the next couple of weeks."

John watched her fold up the bags and put them in the pantry.

For a moment she froze. "Oh, shoot."

"What's the matter?"

"I forgot to get chips and salsa."

"Do you want me to go back to the market and get that for you?"

"Would you mind?"

"No, not at all." Maybe getting away from the house and the ranch would help him shake the blue funk he'd been in ever since that last memory had surfaced. He'd tried his best to make sense of every image that had fluttered past him, but he hadn't gotten a very good handle on any of them, especially that partial, heated conversation between him and a woman.

Instead, he'd felt increasingly unsettled, as though he should be somewhere, as though he had a job to do, as though he might be failing someone. And that didn't sit well with him at all.

And now, here he was, turning off the ignition and heading into the small mom-and-pop-style grocery store to pick up chips and salsa.

As he made his way through the aisles, he found the Mexican food easily enough, but as he scanned the shelves, he spotted a display of Abuelita brand tortilla chips, which sent a good, hard jolt to his memory.

Several images, sights and sounds began to clamor in his mind and he froze in his tracks. As he realized what was happening, he lifted a bag of chips and studied the smiling old woman on the label, her cheeks flushed with pride. And as he did so, a spark of recognition struck.

Rosa Alvarez.

The woman whose recipes and cooking skills had started a company.

A big company.

Jason…Alvarez?

Was that who he was?

He turned the bag over, reading the label. But he skipped over the nutrition facts, instead searching for the processing details: Packaged by Alvarez Industries, San Diego, California.

This was, he realized, the first significant clue he had received. Yet the images were still flickering in his mind like an old nickelodeon that skipped a few photos.

*Find Pedro Salas.*

*Go to Texas.*

But why?

He reached for a jar of salsa—another Abuelita product—and carried it as well as the chips to the checkout stand.

"That'll be eight dollars and forty-three cents," the checker said.

John—no, *Jason*—pulled out a ten and waited for his change. Then he went out to the pickup. But instead of heading home, he searched the area for a pay phone.

He spotted one by the nearby Laundromat and crossed the parking lot to reach it, digging through his pocket for change.

Once inside the booth, he dropped in a quarter, dialed 4-1-1 and asked for the number for the Alvarez Industries corporate office in San Diego. Then, realizing he didn't have enough coins to handle the long-distance charges, he directed an automated operator to place a collect call.

One ring later, a woman answered, "Alvarez Industries. How can I direct your call?"

"I have a collect call from Mr. Jason Alvarez. Will you accept charges?"

"Yes, we will." When the call went through, she said, "Please hold, Mr. Alvarez. I'll get your brother's office."

Too bad Jason hadn't known he had a brother. He blinked a couple of times, hoping it would all come back to him before his brother answered.

"Michael Alvarez's office," another woman said.

Here goes nothing, he thought, as he said, "This is Jason. Can I speak to Michael?"

The woman sucked in her breath. "Oh, my God. Are you okay?"

"Yes, I'm fine."

"Michael isn't in right now. And his cell won't do you any good. The corporate jet was tied up, and he had to take a commercial flight to Denver. He's not due to land for another..." She paused, apparently checking the clock or Michael's itinerary. "Well, he just took off, so it'll be at least two hours. Are you sure you're okay, Jason?"

"Yeah, I'm fine." At least he hoped that he would be—now, anyway.

"David's playing golf at Torrey Pines today with a couple of execs from the J.R. Stein Group. He never takes his cell on the course, so he's not available, either. Can you leave a number so one of them can call you back as soon as they check in with me?"

"Sure." He gave her the number at the ranch.

"Are you sure you're all right?" she asked. "They're going to ask. All they knew was that you went to Texas. But you never checked in."

Was that because of the accident and the amnesia? Or did he have another reason for being away?

Jason didn't want to admit to the woman that he'd been involved in a mugging, that most of his memory was still lost to him. After all, he wasn't sure what kind of relationship he had with his family or why he was in Brighton Valley in the first place.

After the police had questioned the patrons of the Stagecoach Inn, they'd said he was looking for someone named Pedro Salas. But he had no idea why. And because the secretary hadn't mentioned the man or hinted at his quest, he decided to keep that information to himself for the time being.

"I'm fine," he repeated. Hopefully, he'd get more clues after he talked to one of his brothers. "Will you just have one of them call me?"

"Yes, Jason. Of course."

When the line disconnected, he stood outside the market for the longest time, trying to sort through the facts he'd just learned.

But when push came to shove, he still didn't know much more than his name.

## Chapter Ten

Betsy brought her parents home from Shady Glen around four that afternoon. Because her father was a football fan, she left him in the living room watching the Cowboys and Redskins game while she and her mother went into the kitchen.

She waited for her mom to maneuver the walker into the room, then she had her sit at the kitchen table. Whenever possible, she tried to give her mom a job to do, allowing her to feel as though she'd taken part in the food preparation.

Working together had always been a special time between them, whether it was baking cookies as a child or learning how to fix one of her mom's favorite recipes.

Betsy had cooked the hamburger earlier, so all she needed to do was add the seasonings and the tomato sauce, then let it simmer on the stove.

"Will John be eating with us, too?" Barbara asked.

"Yes, he went to pick up some chips and salsa at the market, but he'll be home soon."

If her mother had thought it odd that Betsy had referred to John coming "home," she didn't mention anything, which was a relief.

It's not that she meant to keep any secrets about the two of them becoming lovers, but they really hadn't talked about what the future held for them. How could they when John's past was still in question?

They'd probably get around to it soon, but he'd been a little introspective the past couple of days. And she wasn't sure what was going on with that. Of course, she might be reading something into nothing. And it might be the upcoming holiday that had him pensive.

It was a struggle not to compare him to Doug, though. And she realized that whenever she did so, it was a result of her own past and baggage coming to light.

And speaking of the past, her biological mother's attorney had contacted her again, asking if she'd be interested in a meeting before Christmas. "It would mean so much to her," the man had said.

But Betsy had put it off again. "Maybe after New Year's," she'd said. Then she'd taken the man's number and said she'd call him after Christmas.

"What can I do to help?" her mother asked.

"Do you want to chop tomatoes and lettuce? Or would you rather grate the cheese?"

"It doesn't matter. You choose."

Betsy placed a couple of small serving bowls, a paring knife, the cutting board and the previously washed produce in front of her mother. Then she grabbed the cheese from the fridge and a grater from the drawer.

Dinner would be ready soon. So where was John?

She glanced at the clock on the microwave. He'd left for the market at the same time she'd gone to get her parents.

"Have you decided on a menu for Christmas dinner?" her mom asked. "Turkey might be nice again, even though we had it for Thanksgiving. And I can make that cranberry Jell-O salad again."

Christmas was only a week away, and Betsy had been thinking a lot about the holiday, although she hadn't gotten a tree yet.

"Do you mind celebrating twice?" she asked her mom.

"What do you mean?"

"I'd like to do something special for Doc. And because he probably won't be able to leave the convalescent hospital, we'll have to do it there. But I'd like to have something special at home, too."

John didn't have a family with whom he could celebrate, so she wanted to go out of her way to make it nice for him—and to make him feel as though he was a part of her family.

Who knew? Maybe someday he would be.

Her mother placed the chopped tomatoes into one of the bowls. Then she focused on the lettuce. "Will John be joining us for Christmas?"

"I'm sure he will be." They hadn't actually talked about it, but where else would he go?

"It will be nice to have him with us on the holiday," her mom said. "He seems like a very personable young man."

Personable wasn't the half of it, and the thought put a smile on her face.

As her mother sliced into the lettuce, she asked, "Do you like him?"

Betsy knew she wasn't just talking in terms of friendship. And while she and her mom didn't keep many secrets from each other, her relationship with John was too new and tenuous to make any announcements just yet.

"For what it's worth," Betsy did admit, "John and I have gotten pretty close lately."

"I'm glad to hear that," Barbara said. "Your father and I have been worried about you spending too much time alone."

"I'm pretty busy."

"We love you, honey. And we're enormously proud of the woman and the physician you've become. But you've been *too* busy if you ask us. There have to be other doctors who can cover some of the shifts you've been taking."

Deciding to let that comment slide, Betsy finished grating the cheese and then transferred it into a serving dish that matched those holding the lettuce and tomatoes.

"Are you going to start frying the tacos shells now?" Barbara asked.

"No, I'll wait to do that until right before we eat. In fact, why don't we take some iced tea to Dad and watch the game with him until John arrives?"

"All right." Her mother pulled the walker close to her chair, then slowly got to her feet.

Betsy had no more than prepared four glasses and

carried them into the living room on a tray when she heard Doc's pickup drive into the yard.

"Oh, good," she told her parents. "He's back."

Moments later, John entered the living room with a grocery bag, his expression guarded, his eyes lacking the spark Betsy had grown used to seeing.

Her father stood and extended his arm in greeting, and while John smiled and took the older man's hand, Betsy couldn't help sensing that something was wrong.

"John," she said, as she placed the tray of drinks on the coffee table, "will you please help me in the kitchen?"

"Sure."

When they were out of earshot and alone, she asked, "What's the matter?"

"Nothing."

She crossed her arms, not at all convinced. "You've been pretty quiet lately. And right now, I'm picking up some serious vibes."

"I'm sorry, honey." He blew out a sigh, then brushed a kiss on her brow. "I've had a couple of things come back to me, but not enough to know anything for sure. I think my name is Jason, though. And I'm from California."

"That's it?"

"For the most part."

Something didn't quite jive. Did he remember more than he was telling her?

She didn't know why she thought he was holding back. Something in his eyes, maybe.

"Do you have a last name?" she asked.

"It might be Alvarez. I'm not sure. So far, my thoughts

are pretty scattered. And I'm not ready to talk about any of it yet."

She could understand that—and she could sympathize with it. So, feeling just a bit better, she offered him a smile and gave him a hug. "I'm glad to hear that. I can't imagine how difficult the amnesia is for you."

"Hopefully, it'll soon be a thing of the past."

She sure hoped so. She was just about to suggest that they open the chips and salsa and take it out to the living room when she stole another glance at him, saw his furrowed brow.

He was looking down at the floor, but it clearly wasn't just his boots or the tile pattern that had caught his attention.

Was it something—or *someone*—in California?

Her heart sunk at the thought, yet she didn't think it was fair to quiz him.

When he looked up, he caught her gaze, twisting her heart into a tight little knot. "I'm not going to stay, Betsy. I want to go back to Doc's and be alone for a while. I need to do some thinking."

She could understand that. *Really,* she could. But she sensed him pulling away, just as Doug had once done. And it left her uneasy, her emotions a little too frantic for comfort.

"All right," she said, calling on her professionalism and everything that made her a good doctor. "I'll get dinner on the table. You can eat with us, then take off."

"No." He took a step back. "I'm not in the mood to socialize tonight at all."

Why was that? Was he remembering things that didn't concern her? Things he didn't want her to know?

A chill settled over her as she realized he was shutting her out, just as Doug had seemed to do when their marriage was falling apart.

"Are you coming back later?" she asked. "After I take my parents home?"

"I'm not sure. I've been getting a lot of fleeting thoughts and images, but I can't quite make sense of them. And I think it's better if I just go home where it's quiet."

Go *home?* Just days ago he'd started referring to her house as home. And now he was talking about Doc's.

Or did he mean California?

She couldn't explain just how she knew it, but he was leaving her. And he hadn't even taken a step.

Jason headed back to Doc's place to await a call from California. He'd hated the fact that he'd cut out early on Betsy's dinner party, knowing that it was rude. But he wasn't sure when one of his brothers would call back. And he wanted to be there when it happened.

Fortunately, while he was making a bologna sandwich for dinner, the telephone rang.

He waited a beat before answering so that he didn't appear to be too anxious. "Hello?"

"Jason? Where the hell have you been? We've been worried sick. You flew to Houston to find Pedro, and then that's all we heard."

"I…uh…haven't found him yet."

"But where are you? After not hearing from you for a couple of days, we filed a missing person report. We also sent a private investigator to Texas, and he tracked you to a rental-car company in Houston, but he didn't turn up anything. You never returned the car, and it was reported stolen."

"It *was* stolen."

"By whom?"

"Whoever mugged me and stole my wallet, I suspect."

"Damn. Slow down, little brother. Are you okay?"

"I'm all in one piece, but I suffered a head injury and had amnesia for a while." Actually, he still had it, he supposed. "I seem to be getting my memory back in pieces, so you're going to have to help me out with a few reminders."

"Okay. I'll help any way I can. Have you been able to find Pedro?"

"I don't think so. The problem is, I'm not sure why I was looking for him."

"Damn," his brother said again. "Where are you? I'm going to come out there and take you to the hospital. I want you to have a full evaluation by specialists."

"I've already had one. And I've been under a doctor's care." His thoughts drifted to Betsy, to the hands that touched him in so many different ways. A healer's hands. A lover's hands.

"I'm still going to fly out there," his brother said. "The corporate jet has been getting serviced, but I'll take a commercial flight. Where, exactly, are you?"

"I'm in a small town in Texas. But you don't need to come out here."

"You sure about that?"

Jason wasn't sure about anything, but something told

him he didn't want his brother to come to his rescue. That he'd never needed him to.

"Yeah," he said, repeating himself. "I'm doing just fine. But I have a question for you."

"What's that?"

"Which brother are you?"

The silence over the line was almost deafening. "Are you kidding me? This is Mike. Your oldest brother."

"Oldest of how many?"

"Oh, for cripes's sake. What the hell town are you in? Where's the closest airport?"

"Settle down. I'm fine. *Really.* It's all coming back to me. I'm just trying to piece things together. Can you catch me up to speed?"

Another pause. Then Mike blew out a ragged breath. "Cheryl Westlake filed a sexual harassment lawsuit against me. And a couple of her friends have corroborated her story."

"Is it true?"

"What are you implying?" his brother asked, his tone short, clipped. Annoyed.

"Oh, hell," Jason snapped back, as if used to sparring with the guy. "The lawsuit alone implies that. I just asked whether her charges are true."

"You questioned me about that already, before you flew to Houston. And I'll tell you the same thing I told you then. I didn't fire Cheryl because she wouldn't put out. She wasn't doing her job. She came in late nearly every day, and she couldn't cut it as an HR director."

"So tell me about Pedro Salas."

"He's an alcoholic, and we fired him for coming to

work three sheets to the wind. You don't remember that, either?"

Was that why Jason had been looking for Pedro at the Stagecoach Inn? Had he expected to find the guy crying in his beer?

"It's all coming back to me," he lied.

"Well, if you don't find Pedro, that's fine. It was a long shot anyway. We'll call the attorneys and tell them it didn't pan out. They'll just have to take another approach for our defense."

*Our* defense?

Apparently, Mike's problem had become a family issue, and Jason wondered how he felt about that. Or rather, how the old Jason felt about it. Was he bothered by the inconvenience? Was he ready to battle anyone who attacked the family?

A sense of irritation washed over him. He wasn't sure if it was due to frustration over the fact that his amnesia wasn't lifting as quickly as he wanted it to or if it had something to do with his brother and the dynamics of their relationship.

Time would tell, he supposed. He just hoped he had the patience to wait it out.

"When are you coming home?" Mike asked.

"I'd fly back to San Diego tomorrow, but I'm short of funds. My wallet, my ID and all my cash were stolen."

"Did you cancel your credit cards?"

"Until today, I wasn't even aware of my name. So, no, Mike, I haven't gotten around to it yet." There it went again, the irritation.

"I'll take care of that for you."

"Thanks."

When the call ended, Jason sat in the living room for the longest time, hoping that more of the voices and images would come back to him. But the only thing that came to mind was anger and annoyance at his older brother. And he wasn't sure what that was about.

Twenty minutes later, when the sun had set and the room had grown dark, the phone rang again. And this time, it was another brother who'd gotten the message and was returning his call.

"Hey, Jason. It's David. What's going on? Where are you?"

He gave him the lowdown, and this time, he handled the amnesia news a little better. Or maybe, thanks to Mike's clarifications, the conversation went a little smoother.

"So what do you think?" Jason asked, clearly unable to let go of the questions that had been dogging him. "Do you think there's any substance to Cheryl's allegation?"

"You know how Mike is," David had said. "He's a big flirt and he doesn't always keep his hands to himself or his mouth shut."

"So it's possible that he *did* say or do something that Cheryl could call sexual harassment?"

"Sure, I suppose it's possible. But we're family. So we've got to stick together, right?"

He supposed so.

"Besides," David added, "Mike claims he didn't do or say anything wrong. And I've got to believe him."

Did Jason feel the same way? Until he found some of the missing parts to his jigsaw puzzle, he wasn't sure.

"I'm hopeful that this is all hype on Cheryl's part," David said. "But she's got a couple of former employees to back up her statement."

"And Pedro should be able to testify on Mike's behalf?"

"Before you left San Diego, you told us that you had reason to believe that he'd overheard a conversation that would prove the so-called witnesses were involved in a scam."

But Pedro had been fired for drinking on the job and had moved away, Jason thought, cobbling the pieces he remembered with those he'd been told.

"Did you find him?" David asked.

"No, not yet. But I'll take up the search again tomorrow."

"Good."

Jason gripped the receiver tighter. "So what happens if I don't find him?"

"The lawsuit won't break us. We've got EPLI."

Employer Protection Liability Insurance, Jason realized.

"But the family has always had a great reputation, and no one's happy about the claim, false or otherwise."

That made sense.

A pause stretched across the phone line, and Jason began to think that of his brothers, he might be closest to David.

"Hey," he said. "I've got a question for you. And it's going to sound crazy."

"What's that?"

"Am I married?"

"Not anymore."

"So I'm divorced?"

"Yes. Don't you remember Renee?"

No, but he wanted to. "Just give me a quick recap."

"Okay. Renee Perez. Five-six, a hundred and twenty pounds. Shapely, brunette with green eyes and a great smile, thanks to the set of veneers you paid for."

"Where'd we meet?"

"At a fundraiser held at the polo fields in Rancho Santa Fe."

So was that where he'd picked up his knowledge about horses? At the polo fields?

"You honeymooned in Spain, but once you got home, you went back to work 24/7, just like the rest of us."

Suddenly, the angry woman's voice came back to him, making sense this time. *Those sweet-talking promises of yours aren't going to work on me anymore, Jason. If you go now, it's over. I'll be gone before you get home.*

And apparently, she'd made good on her threat.

"She liked the nice house, the beautiful clothes and all the money you provided her," David added, "but she wanted more of your time."

"And that's why we split?"

"Pretty much. She called you an incurable worka-holic, although it was that dedication to Alvarez Indus-tries that ensured her a pretty damn good settlement."

"So how long have I been divorced?"

"A couple of years."

"Am I dating anyone in particular?"

David laughed. "I've never seen you at any func-tion—business or otherwise—when you didn't have a date. But just recently, you've had the same woman on your arm. She's tall and blonde and, apparently, a lot more understanding than Renee was. I think her name was Katrina."

"Were we sleeping together?" Jason asked.

"I have no idea. You never were one to kiss and tell."

Jason raked a hand through his hair. He didn't have a clue who Katrina was—or what she meant to him. But he wasn't married. That was good news, wasn't it?

Still, he *had* been seeing someone.

After the line disconnected, he continued to sit in silence, thinking mostly.

So now he knew something solid. He was an executive in a successful family business. A divorced workaholic who had no trouble getting dates.

He also lived and worked…and played in California.

What did that mean in regard to his having a relationship with Betsy, a woman who was firmly planted in Brighton Valley?

Could they ever make a life together?

Or would it be best if he just let her go?

Last night, after John left…

Betsy paused in midthought to correct herself. His name was Jason now. She'd have to remember that. But the point she was trying to make was that she'd made excuses for his silence and his retreat to the ranch house.

He was confused by the memories that were returning, she'd explained to her parents. And he needed to be alone.

They seemed to understand why he'd left, and on

an intellectual level, she did, too. He just needed a little time and space to sort things through. Within the next day or so, things would be back to the way they'd been.

But that wasn't true. Something had changed; Jason was different now, and she wasn't sure in which way.

When he'd left her house last night, their gazes had locked, and she'd seen a spark in his eyes, an emotion too difficult for her to decipher. And that's when the remorse had settled over her. That's when she'd faced the truth. And no matter how often she told herself that she was making something out of nothing, that everything would be okay, she couldn't accept that reasoning.

During the last few months of her marriage, she'd made excuses for Doug, too. She'd accepted those long hours he spent at work. And she hadn't questioned all the times she hadn't been able to contact him because he'd supposedly forgotten to take his cell phone with him.

But Doug had also become cryptic and distant at the end, which had made it easier for him to maintain a secret life. And it was that past experience that kept niggling at her now, warning her, preparing her for the worst.

At the end of the evening, she'd taken her parents home and then returned to the guesthouse alone. And even though she'd tried all of her tricks—a warm bath, a cup of chamomile tea—she hadn't been able to sleep.

Around midnight she'd peered out the window toward the ranch house, where several lights lit up the living room as well as the bedroom that belonged to Jason while he was staying with Doc.

The fact that they'd both been awake yet apart left a lump in her chest that lasted throughout the night.

Finally, as dawn spread its fingers over the countryside, she made a decision. She couldn't leave things to chance. She needed to find out who Jason really was, and that meant she would have to be proactive.

So early that morning, on her way to work, she stopped by the sheriff's office. She would ask if they had any news, if there'd been any missing person reports, any stolen cars recovered. After all, Jason had to have gotten to the honky-tonk somehow. Wouldn't it stand to reason that he had a vehicle?

After parking in front of the two-story brick building next to the courthouse, she entered the office.

Deputy Lester Brophy was on duty, and when he spotted her, he got up from his desk near the file cabinets and approached the counter to greet her. "Well, hello there, Dr. Nielson. What can I do to help you?"

"I was wondering if you had any information on that mugging a couple of weeks ago at the Stagecoach Inn. The victim was a man in his late twenties or early thirties, and his injuries landed him in the hospital a couple of days. He's also suffering from amnesia."

"John Doe," Lester said.

"That's the one."

The deputy lifted his hat and scratched his balding head. "I'm afraid there's not much for us to go on. All we found out was that he was asking about a guy named Pedro Salas."

"Do you know who that is?"

Lester shrugged. "Not for sure. Joaquin Salas lives up at Clemson Ridge with his wife and kids. We talked to him, and it seems he's got an uncle by the name of Pedro, but we don't know if it's the guy John Doe was asking about."

"What do you know about him?"

"Just that Pedro lost his wife and his son in a fire about ten years ago. And after that, he went off the deep end."

"What do you mean?"

"Apparently, he's an alcoholic and has a hard time staying employed. Last they heard, he was working in California. He called his nephew after he got fired for drinking on the job and asked if he could come back to Texas and stay with him. But Joaquin told him he'd have to dry out first. And they haven't heard anything else from him."

Betsy leaned her hip against the counter. "What else do you know?"

"That night at the Stagecoach Inn, John Doe got into a tussle with Slim Ragsdale and Bobby Wolford."

"Did he cause the fight?"

"Nope. Slim and Bobby are a couple of troublemakers who've had run-ins with the law on several occasions—vagrancy, disturbing the peace, that sort of thing. But without any witnesses to the mugging, we can't do much about it. And if you talk to Bobby and Slim, they'll try to convince you that they left the bar and went straight to choir practice."

"And that's it?"

Lester nodded.

"No missing person reports?"

"Not in our office or in Wexler. But we've been pretty

shorthanded since Hank Rawlings went out on disability and haven't checked with the other counties."

So Betsy didn't know much more than she already did, other than Pedro Salas had a drinking problem. And he and Jason might both be from California.

"Anything else I can help you with?" Lester asked.

"No, that's it for now. Thanks."

As Betsy started for the door, her shoulders sank under the weight of the answers she'd been given, answers that only served to trigger more questions.

Why would a well-dressed man go into a honky-tonk looking for a drunk? And why would he set off a couple of local troublemakers?

Apparently, whatever keys to Jason's identity lay far away from Brighton Valley. And if she knew what was good for her, she'd get out while she could.

## Chapter Eleven

Jason tossed and turned until about two that morning. And when he finally fell asleep, he didn't rest long. A dream of automobiles crashing into each other, glass shattering and air bags deploying tore into his slumber, shaking him to the core.

But most disturbing of all was that sound of a woman's cries. *Be careful!*

*I'm pregnant.*

*Don't hurt the baby. Please…*

Then she shrieked, as if she were being torn in two, and Jason shot up in bed. His heart was pounding like a runaway train, and his skin was cold and clammy.

"Damn," he uttered, his breaths coming out in short, ragged huffs.

He raked his fingers through his hair and scanned the darkened room, needing to assure himself that the accident hadn't really happened.

Surely the nocturnal vision had only been a figment of his sleep-deprived imagination. But it had been all too real to be sure.

If the goose bumps on his arms had any significance whatsoever, it could be an eerie premonition.

Or had it been an actual memory that had been triggered by the conversations he'd had with his brothers?

He blinked his eyes, trying to recall the details of his unsettling dream.

There'd been an intersection, a blinding glare. A car speeding by. Metal slamming upon metal. Mangled vehicles spun this way and that.

A blonde in her early thirties sat in the driver's seat of a minivan. A jagged gash marred the side of her head, and shards of glass littered her blood-matted hair.

Tears streamed down her face as paramedics and firefighters worked on the vehicle, using the Jaws of Life to cut her out of the crushed metallic prison that held her body captive and refused to let go.

Who was she? The only blonde in his life that he was even vaguely aware of was Katrina, the woman he'd been dating. Was she the injured driver? Was she expecting a baby?

And if so, was it *his* baby?

Is that how Jason figured into all of it?

He might have told his brothers not to worry, that his memory was coming back. But clearly, some things were still lost to him.

Another wave of confusion swept over him as he tried to remember the life he'd once lived.

A sprawling home with an ocean view. A black Mercedes in the driveway. A closet full of suits. A calendar full of meetings and charity events.

Bits and pieces were all he had. But the only life that kept coming back to him, the one that made sense, was the one he'd recently stumbled upon in Brighton Valley. The one he'd found with Betsy.

But if there was a woman he'd been seeing, a woman who might be pregnant, then getting involved with Betsy was wrong. And making love to her, as sweet as it had been, was the last thing he should have done.

His gut clenched at the thought of giving her up, of letting her go. He'd come to care too deeply for her. Hell, he might even love her. But his life was getting more complicated by the minute, and it wasn't fair dragging her into his mess.

Maybe what he needed to do was to go to California, where his life made sense again. Where he could make some decisions based upon fact.

Going back to sleep was out of the question now, so he got out of bed and padded into the bathroom, where he showered. The hot water pounded his neck and back and the steam swirled around him.

As confused as he was, as uneasy as he was about leaving Brighton Valley and all he'd found here, the past was clearly calling him home. Maybe in San Diego, when he was immersed in familiar surroundings, everything would fall into place.

He sure hoped so. The alternative—eternal uncertainty—wasn't going to cut it.

After getting dressed, he went to the kitchen and put on a pot of coffee. While he waited for it to brew, he checked the dialing history and called his brother.

Not Michael, though.

He couldn't explain why or how he knew it, but it was David he went to when he had a problem. David who came to him for the same reason.

His brother answered on the fourth ring, his voice groggy and sleep-laden. "Yeah?"

"David?"

A pause. "Jason? What's up, man?"

"Did I wake you?"

Another pause. A glance at the clock? "Damn. It's three in the morning. I'm not sure where you are, but if it's in Texas, there's got to be a two-hour time difference between us."

Jason blew out a sigh. "I'm sorry about that. I didn't think. I've only been firing on a few cylinders lately."

"What's wrong?"

"I'm coming home, Davey. But I need money."

"You got it. I'll wire whatever you need first thing this morning."

"I'm going to fly home today, too."

"I'll send the corporate jet for you. It was out of commission yesterday, but it should be ready to go today. Where's the closest airport?"

"Wexler, Texas, I think."

"You got it."

"Davey?"

"Yeah?"

"I'm sorry for waking you up."

"Since when?" his brother asked, a hint of humor sparking his sleep-graveled voice. "We've been covering each other's butts for as long as we've been walking and talking."

That was good to know.

*Real* good.

"So how's life in Texas?" Davey asked. "Did you get a chance to play cowboy?"

"Just a little."

"Good. Ever since we moved into the house in Rancho Vista, you wanted to work with horses."

He had?

"Do you remember riding on those equestrian trails near the beach?"

Jason thought for a moment, the memory clicking. Their parents had purchased an estate in an exclusive area near the ocean with two- to five-acre parcels that were zoned for horses. All three of the boys had learned to ride, although their time was also taken up with schoolwork, sports and girls.

"Yes," Jason said, "I remember."

He'd actually tossed around the idea of attending the University of California at Davis and majoring in animal science or something in the agricultural field. But Mike had talked him out of it, saying a business major at USC, their dad's alma mater, was the only way to go for a future executive at Alvarez Industries.

"So what time do you want the jet at the airport?" David asked. "Best case scenario, it's going to be at least nine before they can even take off."

"Let's shoot for about one o'clock my time."

"You got it."

As the call ended, Jason realized that it was a good thing he'd woken up early. He had to get busy if he intended to fly home today.

First, he'd have to hire someone to look out for Doc's

place while he was gone. That would have presented a problem for him, but while he'd been at the feed store yesterday, the proprietor had mentioned that his son was home from college and looking for work over winter break.

The kid's first job would be to drive Jason to the airport in Wexler, although they'd have to stop by the hospital on the way. Jason needed to let the accounting department know that he had medical insurance and that he would forward that information to them shortly. Then he would go up to the third floor and visit Doc.

He was going to thank the man for everything he'd done. He'd also assure him that someone would take care of the ranch while Jason was gone. He wasn't sure when or even *if* he'd be back. But either way, he'd find someone permanent to step in when the student returned to college.

The last thing Jason planned to do was to talk to Betsy. And that visit was going to be tough. He wasn't sure what he was going to say to her. He had to either end things or put their relationship on hold, no matter how much she'd come to mean to him.

But going back to San Diego was his only option, even if he didn't know what it would bring.

Just talking to Davey had caused more of his memories to surface. A picture had begun to form, and it was finally starting to make sense. He'd recalled the closeness he and David had shared, the house on Derby Lane in which they'd grown up, the horses they used to ride.

Everything Jason owned, everything he was—his life,

his identity—was in California. So he had no choice; he had to go back.

He even had a game plan for leaving and seemed to have his proverbial ducks in a row. But that didn't change what he felt for Betsy.

Nor did it make saying goodbye any easier.

The E.R. was pretty quiet, even for a Tuesday morning, so Betsy decided to take advantage of the lull.

She'd just stopped by the break room to pour herself a cup of coffee when Kay Henderson, one of the volunteers, poked her head in the door. "Doctor, there's a guy in the waiting room claiming to be your friend and asking to see you. He says his name is Jason Alvarez, but that you know him as John Doe."

Her heart soared at the news. Had he come to tell her his life had all come together? That he had things to share with her, things that she could pin her heart on?

But she feared that wasn't the case and braced herself for the worst.

After pouring out her coffee into the sink and running the water to rinse it down the drain, she tossed away the disposable cup and went to hear what John Doe aka Jason Alvarez had to say. But once she reached the receptionist's window and spotted him standing near the door, words weren't necessary. She could see the solemn expression on his face.

Whatever he had to say wasn't going to be good, at least not from her perspective. But she may as well get it over with.

"Kay," she said to the volunteer covering for the receptionist, "will you please tell Dawn that I'm going outside for a few minutes. I'll be near the rose garden if she needs me."

"Of course, Doctor."

Then Betsy went out into the waiting room to talk to Jason.

He was wearing a pair of jeans and one of the shirts she'd bought him, which made her think that maybe she was wrong. That maybe he wasn't going to morph back into a stranger.

"I came to tell you that my memory is coming back," he said. "And that I have to leave."

Her heart cracked at the news, but she put on her doctor game-face. "I'm glad to hear that."

"That I'm leaving?"

No. Not that. Yet she forced herself to remain stoical. To pretend that she was giving a patient's family bad news and that she had to be strong, detached.

She nodded toward the entrance. "Let's go outside and talk privately."

"Okay." He followed her out the door, then they turned right and took the sidewalk to the rose garden that provided people with a refuge from the pain and suffering that went on behind the walls of the hospital and a place to pray or meditate.

"I know these past few weeks have been difficult for you," she said, stopping beside one of the concrete benches. "And you must have family and friends who were worried about you."

He nodded. "I don't remember them all. But it's coming back."

*Don't ask about a wife or a lover,* she told herself. *And whatever you do, don't you dare cry.*

"I'm an executive with Alvarez Industries," he explained. "It's a family business."

An executive, she thought. That explained the nice clothing, the education he seemed to have. But it still left a lot of questions, most of which would probably remain unanswered as far as she was concerned.

"I'm glad it's all come back to you," she said.

He skipped over that, saying, "I owe you a lot, Betsy. And I don't know how to thank you."

"You already did." She thought of the memories he'd left her with, the evenings on the porch, the dinner at Cara Mia, the wonderful nights they'd spent making love.

"I've settled up with the accounting office," he added, as if remembering her concerns about the hospital's financial situation. "I gave them my insurance information and an address where they can send a bill for my share of the cost."

"That's good." She stood as tall as her petite frame would allow, even though she wanted to crumple to the ground and bawl her eyes out.

"About the other night," he began.

"Don't give it another thought." She forced a straight face, then felt it weaken when curiosity about his marital status won out. "Unless you found out that you have a wife."

"I did at one time," he said, "but I'm divorced."

She felt momentarily relieved until he added, "But I'm not sure if I'm committed to anyone or not. And until…"

"I understand." A cool breeze ruffled past her, leaving goose bumps in its wake. "But for the record, I'm okay with what we did. We both needed the release."

"Is that all it was to you?" His gaze snared hers, demanding honesty.

But she couldn't be truthful. Not when their lovemaking had been so much more than sex to her. Not when she'd fallen in love with him.

She could kick herself for letting it happen, but she hadn't been able to stop the inevitable.

Her rational side tried to shake some sense into her, insisting that she'd fallen in love with John Doe, a man who wasn't real. That he and Jason Alvarez had very little in common other than the body they shared.

But boy, oh boy, what a body that had been—the olive skin, those blue eyes, that crooked grin. The broad chest, taut abs...

And now that he was standing in front of her, looking every bit like the man who'd held her in his arms, who'd kissed her senseless, who'd put dreams in her heart once again, she felt a wave of remorse at losing him and what they'd once shared, even if he—and *it*—hadn't been real.

Still, her rational side popped up again, explaining why it had happened: she'd needed the respite from her troubles and worries for as long as it had lasted.

Of course, her heart wasn't buying it.

John Doe had made her feel like a woman again, instead of a doctor. And he'd healed something deep within her, even though she should have been the one doing the healing.

And now he was leaving—as Jason Alvarez, a stranger again.

She didn't know what to think. But the sooner she could send him on his way and get control of her life and her emotions again, the better.

"What we had together was good," he said.

Her phony, don't-think-I'm-not-dying-inside smile cracked a little, matching the break in her heart. "But it was never meant to last, Jason. We both knew that."

He glanced at his feet, at the rugged work boots she'd purchased for him when he'd first gone to live on Doc's ranch. And she wondered why he wasn't wearing those Italian loafers and the expensive clothes he'd had on when he came to town.

For a moment, she hoped that he was taking a little bit of Brighton Valley back to California with him. A little bit of...her.

But she'd better get her head out of the clouds and her feet back on solid ground.

When he finally spoke, he said, "I...uh...talked to Doc. And I told him that I lined up someone to look after the ranch until I can find someone a little more permanent to help out."

"You know," she said, crossing her arms to ward off the chill in the air, as well as the painful goodbye. "I had a feeling that you were a take-charge sort of guy."

"I guess you were right."

Funny, but being right wasn't much consolation right now. Not while her heart was crumbling.

"There wasn't any future for us," she added, taking the only position available to her that wouldn't cause her to collapse in a pathetic heap. "The only commitment I need to have right now is one to the hospital and to my patients."

And she'd best remember that.

"I'm not sure when I'll be back," he said. "But we can talk then. Maybe we can have dinner or…something."

Was he trying to let her off easy? Or did "something" mean sex?

If so, she couldn't do that with him ever again. Not when she loved him—whoever the hell he'd turned out to be.

"I'll call you," he said.

Sure, she thought, realizing he'd just left her with the standard last line to use on a date when the evening hadn't gone anywhere.

She lifted her pager and glanced at the screen, as if it had vibrated unbeknownst to him. Then she offered him a wistful grin. "I'd better get back to work. It's showtime again."

But the only show she'd be putting on was this one, the goodbye conversation that was tearing her up inside.

"Okay," he said. "I won't keep you, then. But I wanted to say one more thing."

"What's that?"

"If she asks again, I hope you'll give your biological mother a chance."

"Why is that?"

He shrugged. "Because I think your ex made you wary of being hurt. And because I hope this thing with us didn't make it worse. Sometimes love and relationships deserve a second chance."

She didn't respond, didn't know how to.

As they both headed back to the hospital, he

veered toward the parking lot and she turned to enter the E.R.

On the way, she'd been tempted to blurt out that she loved him, that saying goodbye hurt like hell, but that she understood. And that she wished him well.

But the words jammed in her throat.

When she reached the glass doors of the E.R., she reminded herself that she had more important things to worry about than a crazy, irrational attraction to either John Doe or Jason Alvarez—like wondering if the bank would loan the hospital money to stay afloat until the end of the year. But she couldn't help looking over her shoulder and taking one last peek at the stranger who'd first stolen her heart, then broken it.

And wishing that things were different.


Jason arrived at the Carlsbad Airport at a little after two that afternoon, where he was met by the company limousine.

He'd recognized both the corporate jet, as it had taxied down the runway and stopped to let him board in Wexler, as well as the black luxury vehicle that waited curbside to take him to his house on the beach in Del Mar.

The driver of the limo, a fiftysomething man wearing a sports jacket and a tie, seemed vaguely familiar. He stood beside the open passenger door with his hands clasped behind his back. "Good afternoon, Mr. Alvarez. Did you have a nice flight?"

Jason merely nodded as he climbed into the back of the vehicle. The trip home had been uneventful, but he hadn't felt like talking to either of the pilots or the driver of the car. Leaving Texas had been far more unsettling than he'd expected it to be.

Maybe because that meant leaving Betsy.

After Jason settled into the L-shaped backseat, the driver shut the door, then circled the car and climbed behind the wheel. Before driving off, he looked over his shoulder to peer through the glass panel that separated them. "Where to, Mr. Alvarez?"

"My house. Do you know how to get there?"

"Yes, sir. Of course."

Good, because Jason wasn't sure he could find it just yet.

"Your brother gave me a spare key," the driver said. "He didn't think you'd be able to get in without it."

"He was right."

They drove out of the airport and turned right, heading toward the entrance to Interstate-5.

"I'll bet it's good to be home," the driver said.

Jason didn't respond. The whole trip had been complicated.

He'd been afraid that his leaving would hurt Betsy as badly as it had him, but she'd taken it much better than he'd anticipated.

*What we had together was good,* he'd said.

*But it was never meant to last, Jason. We both knew that.*

But had they?

A part of him wished to hell that what they'd had, what they'd shared, would have lasted. Or that it still had a chance of making it. But before he could stew about her comment, the phone rang.

The driver pushed a button on the dashboard, then answered.

"Hello? Yes, just a minute. I'll let you speak to him." The driver glanced in the rearview mirror. "It's for you, sir. It's your brother. I'll transfer the call to the back and raise the privacy shield."

"But how do I...?"

"There." The driver pointed to a control panel. "It's near the climate control."

"Thanks." Jason waited for the panel to rise, then took the call.

"It's good to have you back," Mike said. "How was your flight?"

"It was okay."

"Did you ever find Pedro?"

"Actually, I stopped at a local honky-tonk on my way out of town." Jason had been wearing the clothes Betsy had bought him so that he'd blend in better with the locals, and he couldn't help thinking that it had brought him better luck. "I talked to a couple of guys who knew Pedro."

"Oh, yeah? Have they seen him lately?"

"One guy seemed to be the spokesman. He wanted to know who I was and what I wanted with Pedro. So I gave him my name and told him we were friends and that we'd worked together in San Diego."

"What'd they say to that?"

"That they'd give him the message."

A beat of silence followed. Then Mike asked, "Do you think he'll call?"

"If he gets the word, he will. We weren't exactly

friends, but we had a connection that went beyond management-employee."

"I told you to watch out and not get too close to your subordinates."

Jason clamped his mouth shut, even though he wanted to snap at his older brother and say, "Look who's talking?" After all, hadn't getting cozy with female subordinates and rubbing elbows—or whatever—with them gotten Michael into trouble?

Not that Jason was saying that he was guilty of Cheryl's charge. But why give people a reason to believe the worst?

"You know," he said instead, "my relationship with Pedro could prove to be helpful."

"I hope that it is."

They ended the call, and Jason glanced out the window, watching the passing scenery, the stretch of the Pacific near the Del Mar racetrack.

He had a turf club membership, he realized. And he spent a lot of time there during racing season. But not because he was a big gambler. He just liked the horses, the people who worked them.

Is that why he'd settled into Brighton Valley so easily? Was that why he wasn't at all happy about coming home?

He suspected that he had an issue with his older brother. That while he loved him and there was a loyalty factor, he didn't always respect him.

Had he always known that? Or had the amnesia and the time away highlighted the things that had been wrong in his life, the things he'd just accepted before because he'd been groomed to be a part of Alvarez Industries?

He wished he had the answer to that, as he settled back into his seat.

Ten minutes later, the limousine pulled in front of a sprawling house on the beach.

*Home,* Jason thought. And while the yard and structure appeared more than a little familiar, he didn't quite feel as though he belonged here.

Was that another result of the amnesia? he wondered. Or was it due to the time he'd spent at Doc's ranch in Texas?

The limousine driver opened the door for him, and as he stepped out of the car, he was handed a key to the house.

"I'm not sure if the alarm is set," the driver said. "If it is, I can't help you there."

That could prove to be a problem, Jason realized. "Would you wait here until I find out? If the police arrive, you'll have to vouch for me."

"Yes, sir."

Fortunately, as Jason let himself in to the foyer, he saw that the alarm was off.

The scent of lemon oil and cleaning products suggested the reason for it. The maid came in a couple of days a week, and he usually left it off for her. He suspected that it had remained off for the entire time he'd been gone.

After waving the driver on, he entered the house and scanned the model-home-type furnishings, with everything in its place.

"Home," he repeated, hoping he would come to believe it.

He made his way to the kitchen, where the breakfast nook window looked out to the ocean.

It was a great view. Did he enjoy sitting at the table or out in the yard? Did he take comfort in the ocean air, like he'd taken comfort in the sights and sounds of the ranch at night?

He cast a glance at the kitchen furnishings, the black marble countertops and stainless-steel appliances. He wandered to the refrigerator and opened it, finding it fully stocked with a variety of beverages.

How about that? Someone had been ready for him.

Katrina? he wondered. Did she come to his house often? Did she have her own key? Had she left her feminine mark on the place?

So far, he hadn't seen any indication that she had.

He was glad of that because he had no inclination to see the woman—no matter what she may have meant to him.

After taking out a cold beer from the fridge, he popped open the flip top, then closed the door. On the counter near the sink, he spotted a telephone–answering machine combination.

A red blinking light indicated he had messages. So he sauntered over to the counter and pushed the play button.

"You have twelve messages," he was told.

Beep.

"Hi, Jason. It's Katrina. Give me a call when you get home. I haven't seen you in a while and thought that it might be nice to have dinner."

Beep. "It's me again, Jason. Where are you? You didn't return my call yesterday. Are you out of town?"

Beep. "Okay, I'm getting worried now. No one at your office will tell me where you are. And you never mentioned leaving. What's up?"

Beep. "I give up, Jason. This is the last call you're getting from me. I realize we don't have a commitment, but common courtesy doesn't cost a dime. Unless you have a very good reason for shining me, don't bother calling back."

Beep. "Oh, my gosh, Jason. I just heard that you disappeared. Are you okay?"

Jason slowly shook his head. Clearly, Katrina wasn't the brightest star in the galaxy. How the hell was he going to call her back if he was missing?

Beep. "Okay, Jason. This is the last call you'll get from me."

Beep.

Beep.

Beep.

He wondered if the hang-ups had been her.

Beep. "Jason, this is Jim Felton, with Felton, Thurman and Grady. Give me a call when you get in. I'd like to meet with you and discuss strategy. Counsel for your insurance company tells me that even though the injuries weren't terribly serious, there's definitely going to be a lawsuit coming down the pike. But the good news is that I spoke to the D.A., and there won't be any criminal charges filed against you for the car accident."

Beep.

He'd caused an accident? The one he'd dreamed about?

The pregnant woman hadn't been Katrina, he realized. She must have been driving the other car. Thank God her injuries hadn't been serious.

As he leaned against the counter, relieved, he was struck by an almost overwhelming urge to pick up the phone and call Betsy, to tell her he'd definitely be coming back to Texas, that he wasn't involved with anyone after all. He just had a few details to work out first.

A *few* details? He had a couple of lawsuits—Mike's and his own—and a formal breakup to a relationship that was already over. He also held an executive board position in Alvarez Industries and all the responsibilities that went along with that.

Damn. Even if he managed to cut strings and smooth out all the rough spots in the road, how could he go back to Brighton Valley and tell Betsy how he felt?

She'd been very clear when she'd told him that what they'd had was nice, but that it was over.

And she'd never even shed a tear.

## Chapter Twelve

After the limousine left, Jason spent the next couple of hours roaming the rooms of his house, scanning the furniture and artwork on the walls and checking out the shelf in the den that displayed a couple of golf trophies he'd won in the various Pro-Am tournaments in which he'd played.

As he did so, some of the spotty memories he'd been having began to weave together, making sense. He knew that Mike was eager to see him, but he found himself dragging his feet. For some reason, he wanted to be clear about who he was and how he fit into the family.

So he went to the refrigerator to find himself something to drink, settling on a can of soda. He flipped open the top, then took a sip as he sorted through a stack of mail on the counter, all of it postmarked prior to his trip to Texas.

His vehicle registration was due in a couple of days.

How many other monthly bills were now outstanding? His post-office box was probably busting at the seams, and playing catch-up wouldn't be easy. He'd have to hire a personal assistant—unless he had one already.

Either way, his first priority was Alvarez Industries, as it always had been.

After placing his empty soda can in a recycling bin, he took a shower and changed his clothes. But instead of choosing one of the many suits that hung in his closet, he picked out a pair of khaki slacks and a golf shirt—considered too casual for the office by Mike's standards. Then he took his car keys from the dresser and went out to the garage, where his black Mercedes was parked.

As he climbed behind the wheel, pictures of the past—some of the conversations he'd had, the people he knew—began to fall into place, providing him with a better understanding of who he was and how he fit into the family dynamics. Thankfully, with each passing moment, his life became more and more familiar.

After backing out of his garage and using the remote to close the door, he drove to the office and parked in his own reserved spot in the underground parking garage. Then he rode the elevator all the way to the top floor and entered the executive offices of Alvarez Industries, where wall-to-wall windows provided an amazing view of the Pacific Ocean on one side of the building and the downtown San Diego skyline on the other.

Suzy Walker, the thirtysomething receptionist, looked

up from her desk and smiled brightly. "Mr. Alvarez, it's good to have you back."

"Thanks. Is Mike in?"

"Yes, and he's been waiting for you. Do you want me to let him know you're here?"

"That's not necessary." Jason was tired of all the formality, which had always felt like a facade to him.

Rosa Alvarez, whose recipes had set up future generations of the family for wealth and success, had been a down-to-earth woman who'd adored her husband and sons. Her smiling face adorned every label, every package, every box of Abuelita brand foods. And while she would be happy to learn of the success of the family business, she'd insist that they all remember just where they came from—hardworking immigrants, loving grandparents, with strong family values.

Jason strode right into his brother's fancy office, briefly addressing Miriam, Mike's executive secretary, yet bypassing her to let himself inside.

Mike glanced up from his computer screen, then brightened. "Jason! It's good to see you, man. I wondered when you were going to get here. I'd thought that you would have Max drive you straight here from the airport."

That might have been Jason's routine in the past, but he'd spent too many evenings in Brighton Valley, listening to horses whinny in the corrals and cattle lowing in the pastures. And he'd enjoyed too many quality hours with a beautiful doctor who dedicated herself to her patients and to the community at large.

Being in Brighton Valley had changed something in him, although he wasn't sure what it was. But he suspected that it had given him reason to believe that life didn't always have to be lived in the fast lane.

"I had some things to take care of at home," he said, realizing those "things" had included getting his memory in check, his feelings sorted and his priorities in line.

"Well, I guess you didn't have time to change. But at least you're here now. Why don't I catch you up on our defense of the lawsuit?"

Jason took a seat in the brown leather chair in front of his brother's desk, then listened as Mike told him the legal game plan.

In a nutshell, if they didn't find Pedro, or if he couldn't dispute Cheryl's testimony, they would have to find some other way to discredit her. And if that didn't work? They'd agree to a settlement and insist that she sign a nondisclosure agreement.

"We can do the same thing with the woman who was involved in your accident," Mike said, "assuming she decides to sue. We'll have the attorneys offer her a settlement so we can put it all behind us."

Jason wasn't the least bit opposed to paying out a fair settlement for an accident he'd caused, but it rubbed against his grain to think that money could easily solve any number of mistakes a man made, any consequences of his poor judgment.

Of course, there wasn't a whole lot that could be done after the fact, other than pay the attorneys and…

What? Make things go away?

How would Rosa and her husband, Luis, feel about that? About the men their descendants had become—business execs, always looking at the bottom line?

Never stopping to smell the roses?

Before Jason could respond, Mike's intercom buzzed.

"What is it?" he asked his secretary.

"Pedro Salas is on the line for Jason. Should I take his number and tell him Jason will call him back?"

"Beautiful," Mike said, brightening and flashing a we're-in-luck smile at Jason before answering Miriam. "Don't put him off. Patch him through."

"Wait." Jason got to his feet. "I'd like to take that call in private."

Mike's brow furrowed, clearly surprised by Jason's response. "Why?"

"I'd feel better talking to him without an audience."

Mike seemed to ponder that for a moment, then shrugged. "Okay. Go ahead. I'll tell Miriam to patch the call through to your desk."

Jason headed out the door and down the hall. When he reached the privacy of his office, he let himself in, closed the door and took a seat behind a large, polished mahogany desk.

Only then did he answer the call. "Pedro, thanks for calling me. How's it going?"

"It's okay. I heard you were in Brighton Valley, looking for me. What's up?"

"I wanted to ask you a couple of questions about a conversation you might have overheard between Cheryl Westlake and a couple of clerks from the mailroom."

Silence stretched across the line until Pedro asked, "What conversation are you talking about? They used to chat a lot whenever Cheryl came downstairs."

From what Jason understood, the woman had been recently promoted, but on her breaks, she would hang out with the clerks who used to work with her.

"Cheryl was talking about a lawsuit against Mike and the company," Jason told him, hoping to jar his memory. "She would have said something to them about sexual harassment."

"Oh, yeah. I remember that. They didn't know I was within hearing distance. Cheryl said she was going to bring your brother down a couple of notches by pressing charges against him."

"What did she claim he did?"

"She said that he was a big flirt and that he came on to every woman between the ages of eighteen and fifty. And that she knew several who'd slept with him, hoping for a promotion or extra perks. But your brother never came through with them. One gal even got pregnant, and supposedly, Mike paid for an abortion."

"Is that true?"

"Hey, all I can tell you is what I heard. But Cheryl seemed to think that just making a claim was guaranteed a settlement. And she told her friends that Mike deserved it, that she was doing every woman who worked at Alvarez Industries a favor by forcing him to be more respectful to his female employees in the future."

Jason couldn't decide if that was good news or not. If Pedro was telling the truth, Cheryl's sexual harassment accusation wouldn't hold up. But it was probably just a matter of time before a legitimate claim was filed. And in that case, Mike was headed for trouble. And so was the family.

"Would you mind testifying to that?" Jason asked.

"We can fly you to California for a deposition or the trial—if it goes that far."

"I really don't want to leave Brighton Valley right now. I'm in a twelve-step program, and it seems to be working."

Jason was glad to hear that. He liked Pedro, and he hoped the guy would find a healthier way to deal with his pain and grief. Thank goodness he'd sought help.

"For what it's worth," he told the man, "we've got those meetings here. And if you stay in the program, I'll make sure that you get your job back at Alvarez Industries."

"That's tempting."

"Give it some thought."

"I will, but I gotta tell you, Jason. It's been really nice being back in Brighton Valley. Life is slower, the air is cleaner and people are more sincere. And to top that off, I've also met a nice lady at one of my meetings. It's not like we're dating or anything, but we've got a lot in common."

"I'm glad to hear that." The poor guy really deserved to find happiness.

"You know," Pedro said, "last night, while I was walking her to her car, we saw a falling star. She said, 'Quick! Make a wish.' And I did. I wished that I could start over again—that I could move past the grief I've been wallowing in for the past ten years and make a new life—in Brighton Valley."

Jason hoped that a change of location and a loving woman could help him change his life around.

After getting Pedro's number, Jason hung up the phone and returned to Mike's office.

"So what did he have to say?" Mike asked.

"His testimony will help. He says Cheryl's just in it for the money."

"Great. I'll make it right for him. Tell him he can have his job back."

"At this point, he doesn't want to come back." Again, that sense of envy struck.

Like Pedro, Jason had found something very appealing about Brighton Valley, but in his case, it went beyond ranches, horses and a more rural lifestyle. It had to do with the people he'd met, the people who'd offered a home and job to a stranger.

People who accepted a man on faith and had treated him like family.

"If he's going to testify," Mike said, "what's in it for him?"

"Maybe some people just want to do the right thing," Jason said. Like Betsy. And Doc Graham.

Jason raked his hand through his hair and added, "That's the trouble with you, Mike. You've got a self-serving agenda, and it's going to be your downfall."

Mike stiffened, as though Jason didn't challenge him often. But all that was going to change.

"That cocky, flirtatious nature of yours is going to get you in one heck of a fix someday," Jason said. "And if you don't change your ways and treat your employees with more respect, some woman is going to lay a claim like that on you, and it's not going to be bogus."

"What's got you on a high horse?"

"I'm just calling it as I see it, Mike."

And that's exactly what he was going to do from here

on out. Life was too short to be unhappy and forced into a role that wasn't of one's own choosing.

Three days later, it was all Betsy could do to keep her mind on her work rather than on her broken heart.

When she moved out of the house she'd shared with her ex-husband, she'd had to deal with a rush of anger and resentment. But she hadn't grieved for Doug's loss. Not like she was grieving for Jason and what they might have had together.

Focusing on her work and on her patients helped, but not when there was a lull in the E.R. On those occasions, she would leave the hospital and get away from people who might ask what was bothering her or why she seemed so sad.

And today was no exception. While the E.R. faced another quiet spell and the waiting room was empty, she'd planned to go for a walk.

But then she'd received an unexpected phone call and was forced to face the past, just as Jason had wanted her to.

"I'll meet you in the rose garden," she'd said, deciding they would need privacy.

But her feet moved slowly, as though a part of her wanted to be somewhere else—anywhere but here.

As she turned the corner, she headed for the stark garden, eager to get the meeting over with. The bushes that had once been lush and full of blooms last spring were bare now, making the grounds look bleak and dreary.

She wondered if coming out here had been a bad idea, especially because this was where she'd last seen Jason. It was a sad reminder of their final goodbye. But there weren't too many places she could go and not risk running into someone.

She spotted a slender, red-haired woman sitting alone on one of the concrete benches, her head bowed. Betsy almost turned around and let her have the place to herself until the woman looked up, and their gazes met.

Betsy's breath caught and she took a step back, thinking she'd just looked into the mirror.

The woman placed a hand on her chest, as if she'd been taken aback by the resemblance, too. She looked ready to bolt, and Betsy could understand that. How often did one run into one's mirror image?

An almost eerie sensation settled over her as she realized she could be looking at her twin instead of her mother. Obviously the woman hadn't been able to take no for an answer.

Betsy had been tempted to return to the hospital and refuse to see her, but Jason's words urged her on. *Sometimes love and relationships deserve a second chance.*

So she put one foot in front of the other, just as she'd been doing to make it through each day after Jason left.

Odd, she thought. The closer she got to the woman, the more of a resemblance she saw.

She supposed she could be a perfect stranger, but the woman had zeroed in on her, too.

"Carla?" Betsy asked, taking a gamble and calling the woman by name.

She nodded as she got to her feet.

"I'm Betsy Nielson."

"I know. I…" Her lips quivered. "I wasn't stalking

you. Honest. I had no intention of bothering you. I just…
wanted to see you." She bit down on her bottom lip.

Betsy didn't know what to say. Their unexpected
meeting had certainly thrown her off stride. But now
that they'd seen each other, now that they'd spoken, she
couldn't very well turn her away.

"I can understand your curiosity," Betsy said. "But
I'm on duty, so I can't promise that I won't be called
back inside."

"I'm not sure if you ever wondered about me, about
why I had to give you up."

"Yes, but I want you to know that I had a happy childhood and wonderful parents. As far as I'm concerned,
your placing me for adoption was a blessing to them,
and I'm glad to be their daughter."

"I'm glad to hear you say that." The wind kicked up,
blowing a strand of her hair across her cheek, and she
swatted it away. "I was a sixteen-year-old foster child
when I gave birth to you, with no real family support.
And your father was in the same boat. As much as I
loved him and wanted to keep you, I knew I'd be sen-
tencing us all to a life we'd never be able to break free
of."

"I understand," Betsy said, figuring the woman
wanted her forgiveness. But there were no hard feelings.
She was happy with the way things had turned out.

"I was an honor student," Carla added, "and a grade
level ahead of the kids my own age. I was looking at a
full-ride academic scholarship to Rice University, but
having a baby would have meant giving it up and getting a job."

"You made a good decision," Betsy said, assuming

that's why it had been so important to find the child she'd given up. "Did you graduate?"

Carla smiled and her eyes misted over. "Yes, with honors. And I went on to get a master's degree in biology. I work for a biotech firm in Houston."

So they didn't just look alike. They had the same scientific aptitude and drive for success.

Betsy took a sip of the coffee she still held. "I guess we have a lot in common. I went to med school at Baylor."

"I'm proud of you, even though I didn't have anything to do with your achievements."

"You gave me to people who cheered me on every step of the way, so we were all winners."

A tear spilled over and slipped down Carla's face, and she managed a smile with quivery lips.

"So tell me," Betsy said, "do I have any half brothers and sisters?"

"Actually, I married Brad—your father. So you have full siblings, not half."

At that, Betsy felt her own eyes water. She'd never had any qualms about her childhood, about having parents who were older than the ones most of her friends had. She'd never really cared that she'd been adopted, although she'd been curious about the details. But she'd always wished that she had a brother or sister, that she hadn't been an only child.

"Brad and I really loved each other, but we wanted more for ourselves and our children than what we'd had. So we waited to get married until after we had our degrees and were established in our careers." Carla reached into her purse and pulled out her wallet. "I have pictures, if you'd like to see them."

Actually, Betsy was intrigued by the idea of having siblings and wanted to see them. "Please."

Carla reached into the photo slots and pulled out a picture of a fair-haired young man with a shy smile. "This is Kenny, your brother. He's a junior at Texas A&M and a math major."

Betsy's heart warmed as she searched for a family resemblance and found it around the eyes and mouth.

"And this," Carla said, as she pulled out a second picture, "is Kari, your sister. She's a senior in high school and far more interested in her dance classes than in math or science. But she's a good kid. And happy."

"I'd like to meet them," Betsy said.

Carla took a breath, as if needing to fortify herself before making a comment. "I'm so glad to hear you say that. Not a day went by that I didn't think about you or pray for you and the family that adopted you. I'm so glad to know those prayers were answered."

"Ten times over," Betsy said. "My parents are wonderful people."

"If you don't mind," Carla said, "I'd really like to meet them sometime and tell them how happy I am that they took you in and gave you all the things your father and I couldn't give you."

"I think that can be arranged."

At that point, Betsy's pager went off, calling her back to the E.R.

"I'm sorry," she said. "I have to go now."

"Thanks for talking to me. Honestly, I would have

abided by your wishes, but I just wanted to see you from a distance. And to make sure that you were happy."

"I am," Betsy said, even though she was nursing a painfully broken heart. But she'd been happy before she met Jason, and she knew she'd be happy again someday.

Before leaving, she reached into her pocket, pulled out a business card and handed it to the woman who'd given birth to her. "We'll have to get together later. After Christmas."

"That's great. And for the record, this will be my best Christmas ever. I've got the gift I've wanted for the past thirty-two years."

Betsy smiled, then turned and walked away.

She was glad that she'd been able to help Carla put the missing pieces of her life back together—even if she hadn't been able to help Jason do the same with his.

Still, with Christmas on the horizon and a new year coming around the bend, Betsy's life was opening up for her in a way she hadn't expected.

She just wished Jason had been around to be a part of it.

As usual, Betsy asked to work on Christmas Eve, something she volunteered to do each year so that the doctors with children could stay home with their families and enjoy the holiday.

She'd even been open to taking the night shift, but Dr. Babbitt had suffered a gall-bladder attack yesterday and had been admitted to the hospital. So she'd taken his shift, leaving the night to Darryl Robertson.

As it neared seven o'clock and the shifts were

changing, Betsy was writing up orders in a patient's chart.

"Dr. Nielson?" one of the nurses asked.

Betsy continued to write. "Yes?"

"There's a man named Jason Alvarez in the waiting room. He's asking to talk to you."

She froze, then forced the pen to finish her thought. "Tell him I'm off at seven. I'll meet him in the lobby."

"All right."

She paused long enough to tamp down her surprise, then she finished out her shift. When she was free to leave, she followed the corridors to the lobby, where she found Jason standing near the Christmas tree, his back to her.

"I didn't expect you to return," she said.

He turned away from the tree, and her breath caught. She hadn't remembered him being that handsome. And she couldn't help noting that he was wearing jeans again. Had he not gone to California after all?

"I needed to talk to you." His expression was solemn and almost unreadable.

She slowly closed the gap between them, yet kept a little distance, like that of acquaintances rather than friends.

"I didn't like the way things ended between us," he said. "In fact, I really didn't like them ending at all."

Her lips parted and her heart thumped to life, but she held her tongue, protecting her thoughts, her feelings.

"I realize there's a lot about me that you don't know, but I was wondering if we could start over from scratch. Maybe, if we dated, it would give you a chance to know the real me."

She wasn't sure what he was asking, what he was saying.

"You made it clear that you weren't looking for a relationship," he added, "and I'll respect that, if you ask me to. But I'd like to see where this goes, and I'm hoping you feel that way, too."

"We live in two different states, Jason. I'm not sure how a relationship could possibly work."

He hooked his thumbs in the front pockets of his jeans and tossed her a crooked grin. "Actually, I just put a cash offer on Doc's ranch, and he accepted the deal. Our attorneys are drawing up the papers as we speak."

He did *what?*

And did that make him her landlord?

Try as she might, she was still speechless.

"I was pretty confused when I left Brighton Valley," he added, "so I couldn't make any promises then. But when I went home, things fell into place."

"And now what?"

"Have you ever heard of Alvarez Industries?"

She hadn't and shook her head.

"What about Abuelita Tamales, Salsa, Tortilla Chips, Mole…?"

"Yes, I've heard of those products."

"My great-grandmother was an incredible cook, and people in the community raved about her tamales. Her husband began to sell them to the neighbors and to his coworkers. And before long, their son began to market them, too, along with her salsa, mole and homemade tortillas. Before long, Alvarez Industries was born."

"That's a *big* company," she said.

"We've been very fortunate. Within three generations, the company went international."

She still didn't understand how a relationship could work out for them. "But you said you were an executive in the corporation. How are we going to deal with the commute?"

"I just resigned from the board of directors."

How could he do such a thing? "Why? I don't understand."

"Before the mugging, I had an almost-obsessive focus on the family business. But something happened while I was in Brighton Valley. I had time to relax, to enjoy life for the first time in years. To be real."

She wanted to take credit for that—or for being a part of the good things that had happened on the ranch, but she knew better than to open herself up for disappointment. So she let her rational side answer. "Vacations can do that for people. The human body wasn't made to work 24/7."

"It was more than that, Betsy. When I was a kid, we had horses. And I secretly considered a degree in animal husbandry. But that wouldn't have benefited my family. So I went to USC and majored in business, just like my brothers.

"After graduation, I went to work at the corporate office and made my own mark on the company. And the fact that sales improved remarkably after I initiated a few ideas of my own made me proud to be a part of a successful, family-owned business."

If truth be told, it made her proud of him, too.

"But I've never really been happy or content. I thought if I just worked harder or put in longer days or made more money…" He clucked his tongue and slowly shook his head. "But it didn't help. I was never as happy or content as I was on the ranch with you. You healed something deep within me, Betsy. Something I hadn't even realized was damaged."

She didn't know what to say. He'd healed something within her, too.

He closed the distance between them and reached for her hand. "I love you, Betsy. Even if you don't feel the same way about me."

"But I *do*," she said. "I was devastated when you left."

"Are you kidding? You were so…"

"Professional? Detached? That's how I deal with stressful situations, Jason. That's one reason I refused to meet my mother. But you were right. Some people deserve second chances."

A smile stretched across his face. "So does that mean you'll give me—us—another chance?"

"Absolutely."

Then she wrapped her arms around his neck and kissed him right there in the middle of the hospital lobby.

After a wonderful night spent in the guesthouse at the ranch, Betsy and Jason celebrated the first part of Christmas Day with her parents in Doc's hospital room. When they arrived, her dad had carried in a miniature tree and set it near the window. And Jason brought in an armful of gifts that Betsy had purchased and wrapped ahead of time.

Of course, she didn't have a package for Jason because

she hadn't expected to share the holiday with him. But his surprise appearance last night and his profession of love had been a prize beyond measure, and the lovemaking that had followed had been an amazing treat.

After Doc had opened his gifts—an iPhone, a new pair of pajamas, DVDs and a book on tape—he apologized. "If I would have known I was going to have a stroke, I would have gone shopping sooner. I'm afraid I don't have anything for you yet."

"Don't worry about it," Betsy said. "Jason and I didn't get each other gifts, either."

"Actually," Jason said, "that's not true. You gave me mine last night, when you agreed to give our relationship a chance. And I've got one for you."

"You do?"

He reached into the lapel of his sports jacket and pulled out a checkbook and a pen. Then, using the table near Doc's bed, he wrote a check.

"I'm sorry," Betsy said. "We'll need to get one thing straight. Cash doesn't count as a present. And gift cards aren't much better. You're going to have to tear that up and start over. I want something that comes from your heart."

"I think you're going to like this one." He ripped off the check and handed it to her.

When she read what he'd written, she furrowed her brow. "Pay to the order of Brighton Valley Medical Center? One million dollars?" She looked up in awe. "Oh, my God. What's this?"

"Something to keep the hospital afloat until things turn around. And hopefully that means a well-deserved vacation for you."

"A loan?"

"No, a gift."

Betsy glanced at the check again. "I don't know what to say."

"A thank-you would work." Jason eased closer and slipped his arm around her waist. "But a kiss would be even better."

She laughed, then threw her arms around him and gave him just what he asked for, as well as a heart full of love to back it up.

Moments later, Jason's cell phone rang and he stepped out into the hall to take the call. When he returned, he was smiling.

"Good news?" she asked.

"The best. Remember the accident I told you about?"

The one he'd caused when he ran the stop sign.

She nodded.

"My father's golfing buddy has a wife who serves on a hospital board. And with her connections, they learned that the child's paralysis wasn't permanent. She'll need physical therapy, but she's going to be okay. And the newborn was released from the NICU a couple of days ago and was sent home. They're all going to be fine, thank God."

They had a lot to celebrate, especially the fact that the accident would soon become a thing of the past. There would be a settlement, but as long as there weren't any permanent injuries, Betsy knew Jason was relieved.

"My mother wants to know when I'm going to bring you home to meet them," Jason said.

Now that the medical center wasn't in dire financial

straits, Betsy would be able to schedule some vacation time. "I'll see what I can do. New Year's Day might be a little early, but I'll put in a request for the first weekend I can get."

John wrapped his arms around Betsy and drew her near. "So Merry Christmas, honey. A new year never looked so promising. We've got a lot to look forward to."

He had that right. They'd both come to grips with the past, and now they could relish the present and look forward to a love-filled future.

## *Epilogue*

Several months later, on a sunny spring day, Jason stood beside his brother David in front of the Brighton Valley Community Church, waiting for his bride to walk down the aisle.

They'd had a rehearsal last night, and he knew right where to stand and what to expect, but that didn't make the waiting any easier. He was eager to see Betsy, to take her hand and marry the woman he loved.

It was nearing two o'clock, and the pews were filled with family, friends and colleagues who wanted to share in the special day. In a matter of minutes, Betsy would walk down the aisle, and they would start their lives together.

After the reception, they would honeymoon in Belize, then they would return to the ranch, where they would make their home and a raise a family. Thanks to Jason's donation, the hospital's financial woes were over, and

Betsy could stay on the day shift and work a normal, forty-hour week.

As the organ began another tune to indicate that the processional would soon begin, Jason watched his brother Mike escort their mother down the aisle, followed by their father. Jason's parents hadn't understood his decision to move to Brighton Valley and buy Doc's ranch, but they respected it. And they adored Betsy.

As his mom and dad took their seats, Barbara Nielson came next, wearing a beautiful green dress she and Betsy had picked out. Barbara couldn't look prettier—or more delighted—as she rode down the aisle in a wheelchair decorated with gold ribbons and white roses. Jim Kelso stood behind her, maneuvering the chair. When they reached the front row, where she would sit, Jim helped her to her feet and get settled in the pew. Then he pushed the chair to the side of the church, out of the way.

Once seated, Barbara glanced across the aisle at Jason's mother. The two women smiled at one another, their eyes misting over.

Betsy's biological family had been invited to the wedding and had taken a back-row seat. In spite of Betsy's fears that meeting Carla would complicate her life, it had turned out to be a blessing instead.

Again, the organ segued to another tune, and Molly Mayfield started on her way to the front of the church, where she took her place as the matron of honor and looked out at those who'd gathered. When her gaze lit upon her husband, Chase, who sat in the third row with their daughter in his lap, she beamed.

As the wedding march began, Jason tried not to crane

his neck, looking for Betsy. When he spotted her on her father's arm, his heart skipped a beat.

Dressed in a strapless, full-length gown, Betsy was a sight to behold. Jason had attended a lot of weddings and seen many beautiful brides, but none of them would ever compare to his.

As their gazes met and locked, he had to tell himself to breathe.

Moments later, Pete Nielson handed his daughter over to Jason, and within minutes, they'd made their heartfelt, lifelong vows to love and cherish each other forever. Then, they shared their very first kiss as husband and wife—sweet and gentle and loaded with promise.

Jason thought his heart would burst with happiness as he led his wife down the aisle.

"You have no idea how happy I am," Betsy whispered.

"I've got a pretty good idea." Jason gripped his wife's hand and gave it a gentle squeeze.

As a camera flashed, his feet slowed, and he turned to her. "Thanks for taking a chance on me when I had no idea who I was."

"It wasn't hard to do. The only thing I didn't know about you was your name. Your strength, your honesty, your integrity, were all there. All I had to do was open my heart and let you in."

There, in the back of the church, he gave her another kiss—this one spontaneous and unrehearsed.

*I love you,* it promised. *Today, tomorrow and always.*

\* \* \* \* \*

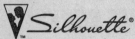

# COMING NEXT MONTH

## Available November 30, 2010

SPECIAL EDITION

# REQUEST YOUR FREE BOOKS!
## 2 FREE NOVELS PLUS 2 FREE GIFTS!

# SPECIAL EDITION
### Life, Love and Family!

**YES!** Please send me 2 FREE Silhouette® Special Edition® novels and my 2 FREE gifts (gifts are worth about $10). After receiving them, if I don't wish to receive any more books, I can return the shipping statement marked "cancel." If I don't cancel, I will receive 6 brand-new novels every month and be billed just $4.24 per book in the U.S. or $4.99 per book in Canada. That's a saving of 15% off the cover price! It's quite a bargain! Shipping and handling is just 50¢ per book.* I understand that accepting the 2 free books and gifts places me under no obligation to buy anything. I can always return a shipment and cancel at any time. Even if I never buy another book from Silhouette, the two free books and gifts are mine to keep forever.

235/335 SDN E5RG

Name _____ (PLEASE PRINT) _____

Address _____ Apt. # _____

City _____ State/Prov. _____ Zip/Postal Code _____

Signature (if under 18, a parent or guardian must sign) _____

### Mail to the Silhouette Reader Service:
**IN U.S.A.:** P.O. Box 1867, Buffalo, NY 14240-1867
**IN CANADA:** P.O. Box 609, Fort Erie, Ontario L2A 5X3

Not valid for current subscribers to Silhouette Special Edition books.

**Want to try two free books from another line?**
**Call 1-800-873-8635 or visit www.morefreebooks.com.**

* Terms and prices subject to change without notice. Prices do not include applicable taxes. N.Y. residents add applicable sales tax. Canadian residents will be charged applicable provincial taxes and GST. Offer not valid in Quebec. This offer is limited to one order per household. All orders subject to approval. Credit or debit balances in a customer's account(s) may be offset by any other outstanding balance owed by or to the customer. Please allow 4 to 6 weeks for delivery. Offer available while quantities last.

**Your Privacy:** Silhouette is committed to protecting your privacy. Our Privacy Policy is available online at www.eHarlequin.com or upon request from the Reader Service. From time to time we make our lists of customers available to reputable third parties who may have a product or service of interest to you. If you would prefer we not share your name and address, please check here. ☐

**Help us get it right**—We strive for accurate, respectful and relevant communications. To clarify or modify your communication preferences, visit us at www.ReaderService.com/consumerchoice.

SSE10R

*See below for a sneak peek from our classic
Harlequin® Romance® line.*

**Introducing DADDY BY CHRISTMAS by Patricia Thayer.**

MIA caught sight of Jarrett when he walked into the open lobby. It was hard not to notice the man. In a charcoal business suit with a crisp white shirt and striped tie covered by a dark trench coat, he looked more Wall Street than small-town Colorado.

Mia couldn't blame him for keeping his distance. He was probably tired of taking care of her.

Besides, why would a man like Jarrett McKane be interested in her? Why would he want to take on a woman expecting a baby? Yet he'd done so many things for her. He'd been there when she'd needed him most. How could she not care about a man like that?

Heart pounding in her ears, she walked up behind him. Jarrett turned to face her. "Did you get enough sleep last night?"

"Yes, thanks to you," she said, wondering if he'd thought about their kiss. Her gaze went to his mouth, then she quickly glanced away. "And thank you for not bringing up my meltdown."

Jarrett couldn't stop looking at Mia. Blue was definitely her color, bringing out the richness of her eyes.

"What meltdown?" he said, trying hard to focus on what she was saying. "You were just exhausted from lack of sleep and worried about your baby."

He couldn't help remembering how, during the night, he'd kept going in to watch her sleep. How strange was that? "I hope you got enough rest."

She nodded. "Plenty. And you're a good neighbor for

coming to my rescue."

He tensed. Neighbor? *What neighbor kisses you like I did?* "That's me, just the full-service landlord," he said, trying to keep the sarcasm out of his voice. He started to leave, but she put her hand on his arm.

"Jarrett, what I meant was you went beyond helping me." Her eyes searched his face. "I've asked far too much of you."

"Did you hear me complain?"

She shook her head. "You should. I feel like I've taken advantage."

"Like I said, I haven't minded."

"And I'm grateful for everything…"

Grasping her hand on his arm, Jarrett leaned forward. The memory of last night's kiss had him aching for another. "I didn't do it for your gratitude, Mia."

*Gorgeous tycoon Jarrett McKane has never believed in Christmas—but he can't help being drawn to soon-to-be-mom Mia Saunders! Christmases past were spent alone…and now Jarrett may just have a fairy-tale ending for all his Christmases future!*

*Available December 2010, only from Harlequin® Romance®.*

HARLEQUIN *Presents*

Bestselling Harlequin Presents® author

# Julia James

*brings you her most powerful book yet...*

# FORBIDDEN OR FOR BEDDING?

### *The shamed mistress...*

Guy de Rochemont's name is a byword for wealth and power—and now his duty is to wed.

Alexa Harcourt knows she can never be anything more than *The de Rochemont Mistress*.

But Alexa—the one woman Guy wants—is also the one woman whose reputation forbids him to take her as his wife....

## Available from Harlequin Presents December 2010

www.eHarlequin.com

HP12960